THE
IMPORTANCE OF
BEING EARNEST

THE
IMPORTANCE OF
BEING EARNEST

Oscar Wilde

An imprint of Om Books International

First published in 2018

Om
KIDZ | Om Books International

Corporate & Editorial Office
A-12, Sector 64, Noida 201 301
Uttar Pradesh, India
Phone: +91 120 477 4100
Email: editorial@ombooks.com
Website: www.ombooksinternational.com

Sales Office
107, Ansari Road, Darya Ganj
New Delhi 110 002, India
Phone: +91 11 4000 9000
Email: sales@ombooks.com
Website: www.ombooks.com

© Om Books International 2018

Adapted by Swayam Ganguly

ISBN: 978-93-85031-67-0

Printed in India

10 9 8 7 6 5 4 3 2 1

Contents

1.	Act One	7
2.	Act Two	83
3.	Act Three	181
	About The Author	238
	Characters	239
	Questions	240

Act One

Scene: *Morning-room in Algernon's flat in Half-Moon Street, London, W.*

Time: *The present. The room is furnished tastefully, artistically, and luxuriously. The sound of a piano resonates from the adjoining room.*

Lane *is busy arranging afternoon tea on the table, and after the music has stopped playing,* **Algernon** *enters.*

Algernon: Lane, did you happen to hear what I was playing?

Lane: I thought it would be polite not to listen, sir.

Algernon: Well, I am sorry for that, for your sake, Lane. Agreed, I am not the most accurate musician. Why, anyone can play accurately

for that matter. But what I do play with, is wonderful expression. Sentiment is my forte as far as the piano is concerned. Science is something I keep reserved for Life.

Lane: Yes, sir.

Algernon: Speaking of the science of Life, have you managed to get the cucumber sandwiches cut for Lady Bracknell?

Lane: Yes, sir. (*Hands them on a salver.*)

Algernon (*inspects them, takes two, and sits down on the sofa*): Oh!...by the way, Lane, I arrived at the conclusion by studying your book that eight bottles of champagne have been entered as having been consumed on Thursday night, when Lord Shoreman and Mr. Worthing dined with me last.

Lane: Yes, sir; eight bottles and a pint.

Algernon: Tell me something. Why is it that the servants always drink the champagne at a bachelor's house? I ask merely for information.

Lane: I think it is because of the superior quality

of the wine, sir. I have often observed that the champagne in married households is usually not of a first-rate brand.

Algernon: Good heavens! Can marriage be as demoralising as that?

Lane: I do believe it to be a pleasant state sir. I have had very little experience of it, having been married only once. That was because of a misunderstanding between myself and a young person.

Algernon (*languidly*): I don't know if your family life interests me much, Lane.

Lane: No, sir; it is not an interesting subject. I do not think of it myself.

Algernon: That's natural, I am sure. That will do, Lane, thank you.

Lane: Thank you, sir.

Lane *exits.*

Algernon: Lane's views on marriage are somewhat slack. If the lower orders do not set us a good example, what use do we have for them? As a class, they appear to have absolutely no sense of moral responsibility.

Enter **Lane**.

Lane: Mr. Ernest Worthing.

Enter **Jack**. **Lane** *exits*.

Algernon: How are you, my dear Ernest? What brings you up to town?

Jack: Pleasure! What else can bring one anywhere? Eating as usual, I see Algy!

Algernon (stiffly): I believe it is the custom of good society to take some slight refreshment at five o' clock. But where have you been since last Thursday?

Jack (*sitting down on the sofa*): In the country.

Algernon: What on earth do you do there?

Jack (pulling off his gloves): One amuses oneself when one is in town. But one amuses others when one is in the country, which is rather boring.

Algernon: Who are these people that you amuse?

Jack (airily): Oh, neighbours.

Algernon: Got nice neighbours in your part of Shropshire?

Jack: Absolutely horrid! I don't speak to any one of them.

Algernon: How much you must amuse them then! (*Walks over and takes a sandwich.*) By the way, Shropshire is your country, is it not?

Jack: Eh? Shropshire? Yes, of course. Hallo! Why so many cups? Why cucumber sandwiches? Why such reckless extravagance in someone so young? Who is coming to tea?

Algernon: Oh! Merely Aunt Augusta and Gwendolen.

Jack: How perfectly delightful!

Algernon: Yes, but I'm afraid Aunt Augusta won't quite approve of your being here.

Jack: May I ask why?

Algernon: Well, the way you flirt with Gwendolen is totally disgraceful. Why, it is almost as bad as the way she flirts with you.

Jack: Algy, I am in love with Gwendolen. I have come to town especially to propose to her.

Algernon: I call that business. I thought you

had come up for pleasure.

Jack: You are utterly unromantic!

Algernon: You see, I fail to see anything romantic in proposing. It is very romantic to be in love, but there is nothing romantic about a definite proposal. One might be accepted, and usually is, I believe. Then, the excitement ends. The very essence of romance is uncertainty. If I ever get married, I shall certainly try to forget the fact.

Jack: I have no doubt about that, dear Algy. The Divorce Court was specially invented for people with such curious memories.

Algernon: Oh! Speculation on such a subject is useless. Divorces are made in heaven------ (**Jack** *puts out a hand to take a sandwich and Algernon interferes instantly.*) Please don't touch the cucumber sandwiches as they have been ordered specifically for Aunt Agatha. (*Takes one and eats it himself*)

Jack: Well, I see you've been eating them all the time.

Algernon: That is a different matter altogether. You see, she is my aunt. Help yourself to some bread and butter. That's for Gwendolen who is absolutely devoted to bread and butter.

Jack: (*helping himself to some bread and butter*): That's very good bread and butter.

Algernon: My dear fellow, do not eat it as if you are going to eat it all. You behave as if you are already married to Gwendolen. You are not, and I think you will never be.

Jack: What on earth makes you assume that?

Algernon: Well, firstly, girls never marry the men they flirt with. They don't think it to be right.

Jack: Oh, that's nonsense!

Algernon: It's not! It's a great truth. It explains the numerous bachelors one sights all over the place. Secondly, I refuse to give my consent on the matter.

Jack: Your consent!

Algernon: Well, Gwendolen is my first cousin, my dear fellow. Before I permit you to marry her, you must clear up the whole question of Cecily, my dear chap.

Jack: Cecily? What on earth do you mean, Algy? I don't know anyone called Cecily.

Enter **Lane**

Algernon: Lane, bring me the cigarette case Mr. Worthing left behind in the smoking-room the last time he dined here.

Lane: Yes, sir

Lane *exits*.

Jack: Do you mean to say that you had my cigarette case all this time? I have been writing letters frantically to Scotland Yard about it. Why, I was on the verge of offering a large reward.

Algernon: I wish you would offer one. I happen to be unusually hard up and could use the money.

Jack: There is no point offering a large reward now that it has been found.

Enter **Lane** *with the cigarette case on a salver.*
Algernon *takes it at once.* **Lane** *exits.*

Algernon: I think that is rather mean of you, Ernest. (*Opens case and examines it.*) Now that I look at the inscription inside, I discover that this thing does not really belong to you after all.

Jack: Of course it's mine, Algy. (*Moving towards him*) You have seen me with it a hundred times, and you have no right whatsoever to read what is written inside. It is not a gentlemanly thing to read a private cigarette case.

Algernon: It is absurd to observe a hard and fast rule about what one should read and what one shouldn't. More than half of modern culture is dependent upon what one shouldn't read.

Jack: I am well aware of the fact, and I do not propose to discuss modern culture as it is not the sort of matter to be talked of privately. I simply want my cigarette case back.

Algernon: But this isn't your cigarette case. It

is a present from someone named Cecily, and you said you didn't know anyone of that name.

Jack: If you really want to know, Cecily happens to be my aunt!

Algernon: Your aunt!

Jack: Yes, charming lady she is, too. She lives at Tunbridge Wells. Just give it back to me, Algy.

Algernon (*retreating to the back of the sofa*): But why does she call herself little Cecily if she is your aunt? (*Reading*) "From little Cecily with her fondest love."

Jack (*moving to sofa and kneeling upon it*): My dear fellow, what is there in that? You know how some aunts are tall, and some aunts are short. Don't you think that such a matter must surely be allowed to be decided by the aunt herself? Why do you think that every aunt should be exactly like your aunt? That is an absurd thing to assume! For Heaven's sake, return my cigarette case at once. (*Follows him around the room.*)

Algernon: But why does your aunt call you her uncle? "From little Cecily, with her fondest love to her dear Uncle Jack." There is no objection to an aunt being small in size, but why an aunt should address her nephew as her uncle is something that I cannot figure out. Besides, your name is not Jack at all; it is Ernest. How do you explain that?

Jack: It isn't Ernest; it's Jack.

Algernon: I have always known you as Ernest as you have always told me that it was your name. I have introduced you to everyone as Ernest. You look like your name was Ernest, and you reply to the name Ernest. You are the most earnest-looking person that I have ever seen in my life. There cannot be anything more absurd than your saying that your name is not Ernest and something else now. That name is on your cards. (*Taking one from the case.*) "Mr. Ernest Worthing, B.4, The Albany." I'll keep this as evidence that your name is Ernest if you ever attempt to deny it to me, or to Gwendolen, or to anyone else. (*Puts the card in his pocket.*)

Jack: Well, my name is Ernest in town, and Jack in the country. The cigarette case was given to me in the country.

Algernon: Yes, but that does not account for the fact that your small aunt Cecily, residing at Tunbridge Wells, calls you her dear Uncle. Come, old boy, you had much better tell me the truth at once.

Jack: My dear Algy, you speak just like a dentist. It is rather vulgar to speak like a dentist when one is not a dentist. It does give a false impression, you know.

Algernon: Well, that is precisely what dentists always do. Go on, now! Tell me the whole story. I must say that I have always suspected you of being a confirmed and secret Bunburyist. Now, I am absolutely positive that you are one.

Jack: Bunburyist? What on earth do you mean by that?

Algernon: I shall reveal to you the meaning of that unparalleled expression as soon as you are kind enough to explain to me why you are Ernest in town and Jack in the country.

Jack: Give me back my cigarette case first.

Algernon: Here it is. (*Hands cigarette case.*) Now give me your explanation, and please don't make it improbable. (*Sits on the sofa.*)

Jack: My dear Algy, I'm afraid there is nothing improbable about my explanation at all. On the other hand, it is perfectly ordinary. Old Mr. Thomas Cardew adopted me when I was a little boy. In his will, he made me the guardian to his granddaughter, Miss Cecily Cardew. Cecily addresses me as her uncle from such respect that could not be possibly appreciated by you. She lives at my place in the country under the charge of her able and admirable governess, Miss Prism.

Algernon: Where is this place in the country, by the way?

Jack: That is nothing to you, dear fellow. You are not going to be invited there. But I must tell you candidly that the place is not near Shropshire.

Algernon: I suspected that already as I have Bunburyed all over Shropshire on two separate occasions. Now, carry on! You still haven't explained to me why you are Ernest in town, and Jack in the country.

Jack: My dear Algy, I am unsure if you will be able to comprehend my real motives in doing so. You are barely serious enough. When a man is placed in the position of a guardian, as I have, the adoption of a very high moral tone on all subjects becomes essential. It is one's duty to behave in such a manner. But a high moral tone, it must be said, hardly is conducive to one's health or one's happiness. Hence, whenever I have come to town, I have always pretended to be an imaginary younger brother by the name of Ernest, who lives in the Albany, and gets into the most dreadful scrapes. That, my dear Algy, is the whole, pure, and simple truth.

Algernon: The truth is rarely pure and never simple. Modern life would be very tedious if either of the two were like that. Modern literature would be an impossibility as well.

Jack: Well, that wouldn't be such a bad thing at all.

Algernon: My dear fellow, literary criticism is not your forte. So, do not attempt it. You should leave that to people who haven't attended a University. They do it so well at the daily papers. What you really are is a Bunburyist, and I was quite right in assuming that you were one. In fact, you are one of the most advanced Bunburyists I know.

Jack: What on earth do you mean, Algy?

Algernon: Well, you have invented a younger brother called Ernest who's rather useful, so that you can come up to town as often as you like. Likewise, I have invented an invaluable permanent invalid called Bunbury, so that I can go down to the country whenever I wish to. For instance, if it were not for Bunbury's bad health, I wouldn't be unable to dine with you at Willis's tonight, for I have been really engaged for this appointment with Aunt Agatha for more than a week.

Jack: I haven't asked you to dine with me tonight.

Algernon: I know that. It is rather foolish of you not to send out invitations. You are absolutely careless about that. Nothing annoys people more than not to receive invitations.

Jack: You should dine with your Aunt Agatha.

Algernon: I haven't the smallest intention of doing that. I dined there on Monday, and once a week is rather enough to dine with one's relations. Secondly, whenever I dine at Aunt Agatha's, I am always treated as a member of the family. I am sent down with either no woman at all, or two of them. Thirdly, I'm

perfectly aware whom she will place me next to at dinner tonight. I shall be placed next to Mary Farquhar, who always flirts with her own husband across the dinner-table. Now, this sort of thing is rapidly on the rise, and the amount of women in London who flirt with their own husbands is absolutely scandalous. It looks bad just like washing one's dirty linen in public. Also, as I know you to be a confirmed Bunburyist, it is but natural that I want to talk to you about Bunburying. I want to tell you all the rules.

Jack: Now, listen, I'm not a Bunburyist at all. I am going to kill my imaginary brother if Gwendolen accepts me. I think I'm going to kill him in any case as even Cecily is interested in him a little too much, even without meeting him even once. It is rather a bore. So, I'm going to get rid of Ernest. I would also advise you strongly to get rid of your invalid friend, Mr.......... the one with that absurd name.

Algernon: Nothing on earth would induce me to part with Bunbury, and you will be glad to know him if you ever get married, which at the moment appears rather problematic to me. A man who marries without knowing Bunbury has a rather tedious time of it.

Jack: That is nonsense, Algy. If I marry a charming girl like Gwendolen, and she is the only girl in the world I would like to marry, I would definitely not want to know Bunbury.

Algernon: Then your wife will. You don't seem to realise, that in married life three is company and two is none.

Jack: That theory has been driven into your head by the corrupt French drama for the last fifty years, my dear young friend.

Algernon: Yes; the happy English home has proved the theory half the time.

Jack: Don't try to be cynical, for heaven's sake. It is perfectly easy to be cynical.

Algernon: It isn't easy to be anything nowadays,

my dear fellow. There's such a lot of beastly competition about. (*The sound of an electric bell is heard*) Ah! That must be Aunt Augusta. Only relatives or creditors, are capable of ringing in that Wagnerian manner. Now, suppose I get her out of the way for ten minutes, so you are provided the opportunity of proposing to Gwendolen, may I dine with you tonight at Willis's?

Jack: I suppose so, if you want to.

Algernon: Yes, but you must be serious about dinner. I hate people who are not serious about meals. It is so shallow of them.

Enter **Lane**.

Lane: Lady Bracknell and Miss Fairfax.

Algernon goes forward to receive the ladies.

Enter **Lady Bracknell** and **Gwendolen**.

Lady Bracknell: Good afternoon, dear Algernon, I hope you are behaving very well.

Algernon: I'm feeling very well, Aunt Augusta.

Lady Bracknell: Well, that's not quite the same thing. In fact, the two things rarely go together.

(*Sees* **Jack** *and bows to him with icy coldness.*)

Algernon (*to* **Gwendolen**): Dear me, you are smart!

Gwendolen: I am always smart! Am I not, Mr. Worthing?

Jack: You're quite perfect, Miss Fairfax.

Gwendolen: Oh! I hope I am not that. It would leave no room for further developments then, and I intend to develop in many directions.

(**Gwendolen** *and* **Jack** *sit down together in the corner.*)

Lady Bracknell: I am sorry we are a little late, Algernon, but I was obliged to call on dear Lady Harbury. I hadn't been to her place since her poor husband's death. I have never seen a woman so altered as she looks twenty years younger now. Now, I'll have a nice cup of tea, and one of those nice cucumber sandwiches you promised me.

Algernon: Certainly, Aunt Augusta. (*Goes over to tea-table.*)

Lady Bracknell: Won't you come and sit here, Gwendolen?

Gwendolen: Thanks, mamma, I'm quite comfortable here.

Algernon: (*picking up empty plate in horror*): Good heavens! Lane! Where are the cucumber sandwiches? I had them ordered specially.

Lane: There were no cucumbers in the market this morning, sir. I went down twice.

Algernon: No cucumbers!

Lane: No, sir. Not even for ready money.

Algernon: That will do, Lane. Thank you.

Lane: Thank you, sir. (*Exits.*)

Algernon: I am very distressed, Aunt Augusta, about the fact that there are no cucumbers available, even with ready money.

Lady Bracknell: It really does not matter, Algernon. I had some crumpets with Lady Harbury. She appears to me to be living entirely for pleasure now.

Algernon: Her hair has turned gold from grief, I hear.

Lady Bracknell: Well, it certainly has changed its colour. The cause, however, is unknown to me. (**Algernon** *offers tea.*) Thank you. I have quite a treat for you tonight, Algernon. I am going to send you down with Mary Farquhar. She is such a nice woman, and so attentive towards her husband. It is such a delight to watch them together.

Algernon: Aunt Augusta, I am afraid that I have to give up the pleasure of dining with you tonight.

Lady Bracknell (*frowning*): I hope not, Algernon. That would put my table completely out. Your uncle would have to dine upstairs. Thankfully, he is accustomed to that.

Algernon: Needless to say, it is indeed a terrible disappointment to me. But I've just received a telegram stating that my poor friend Bunbury is very ill again. (*Exchanges looks with Jack*) They

are of the opinion that I should be with him.

Lady Bracknell: That is very strange. This Mr. Bunbury always seems to suffer from curiously bad health.

Algernon: Yes, poor Bunbury is a dreadful invalid.

Lady Bracknell: I must say, Algernon, that I think it is high time that Mr. Bunbury made up his mind whether he wants to stay alive or die. This shilly-shallying with the matter is absurd. I do not in any way approve of this modern sympathy with invalids. In fact, I think it is morbid. I think illness of any kind is hardly a thing to be encouraged in others. Health, after all, is the primary duty of life. I am always saying so to your poor uncle, but he never seems to take much notice....as far as if there is any improvement in his ailment. I should be much obliged if you can ask Mr. Bunbury on my behalf, to be kind enough not to have a relapse on Saturday. This is because I am relying on you to arrange my music for me. It is my last reception, and I want something that will encourage conversation, especially at the end of the season when everyone has practically said whatever it is that they wished to say, which in most cases, was probably not much.

Algernon: I'll have a word with Bunbury, Aunt Augusta, provided he is still conscious, and I think I can promise you that he will be all right on Saturday. Then again, the music is a great difficulty. You see, if one plays good music, people do not tend to listen, and people do not converse if bad music is played. But I shall run over the programme I've drawn out, if you will kindly come into the next room for a moment.

Lady Bracknell: Thank you, Algernon. That is indeed very thoughtful of you. (*Rising and following* **Algernon**.) I am sure the programme will be delightful. I cannot possibly allow French songs though, as people always seem to think of them as improper. They either look shocked, which is vulgar, or laugh, which is even worse. German, on the other hand, sounds a thoroughly respectable language, and I also believe it to be so. Gwendolen, please accompany me.

Gwendolen: Certainly, mamma.

Lady Bracknell *and* **Algernon** *enter the music room,* **Gwendolen** *remains behind.*

Jack: Charming day, Miss Fairfax.

Gwendolen: Pray don't talk to me about the weather, Mr. Worthing. I am certain people mean something else when they talk to me about the weather. That makes me so nervous.

Jack: I do mean something else.

Gwendolen: I thought as much. In fact, I am never wrong.

Jack: I would like to be allowed to take advantage of Lady Bracknell's temporary absence…

Gwendolen: I would certainly advise you to do so. But Mamma has a way of re-entering a room that I have often had to speak to her about.

Jack (*nervously*): Miss Fairfax, I have admired

you more than any other girl...I have met...
ever since I have met you.

Gwendolen: Yes, I am well aware of the fact.
But I often wish that you had been more
demonstrative about it in public. I know that
you have always had an irresistible fascination
for me. Even before I had met you, I was
not indifferent to you. (**Jack** *stares at her in
amazement*) We live in an age of ideals, Mr.
Worthing, as you are aware hopefully. This
fact is constantly mentioned in the expensive
monthly magazines, and I am told has now
reached the provincial pulpits. My ideal has
always been to love someone named Ernest.
There is something in the name Ernest that
inspires absolute confidence. The moment
Algernon mentioned he had a friend named
Ernest, I knew it was my destiny to love you.

Jack: Do you really love me, Gwendolen?

Gwendolen: Passionately!

Jack: Darling! You have no idea how happy you've made me.

Gwendolen: My own Ernest!

Jack: But you don't really mean to say that you wouldn't love me if my name wasn't Ernest?

Gwendolen: But your name is Ernest.

Jack: Yes, I know it is. But suppose if it was something else? Do you mean to say you wouldn't love me then?

Gwendolen (*glibly*): That is clearly a metaphysical speculation, and like most metaphysical speculations has very little reference to the actual facts of real life, as known to us.

Jack: Personally speaking darling, and candidly as well, I don't care much about the name Ernest...I don't think it suits me at all.

Gwendolen: It suits you perfectly. It is a divine name. It has a music of its own that produces vibrations. Ernest!

Jack: But really, Gwendolen, I think there are lots of other names that are nicer. For instance,

I think Jack is a charming name.

Gwendolen: Jack? No, there is little music in the name Jack, if at all there is. It does not thrill, and produces no vibrations absolutely. I have known many Jacks, and all of them were more than usually plain. Jack is also a notorious domesticity for John! I absolutely pity any woman married to a man named John. She would probably not experience the entrancing pleasure of even a single moment's solitude. The only safe name is Ernest, really.

Jack: Gwendolen, I must get christened at once-I mean we must get married at once. There is no time to be lost.

Gwendolen: Married, Mr. Worthing?

Jack (*astounded*) Well…surely. You know that I love you, and Miss Fairfax, you have led me to believe that you are not absolutely averse to the idea.

Gwendolyn: I adore you. But you haven't proposed to me yet. We haven't even spoken

about marriage and the subject hasn't been touched upon.

Jack: May I propose to you now?

Gwendolen: I think it would be a suitable opportunity, and to spare you any kind of disappointment, Mr. Worthing, let me frankly tell you beforehand that I'm quite determined to accept you.

Jack: Gwendolen!

Gwendolen: Yes, Mr. Worthing, what do you have to say to me?

Jack: You know very well what I have to say to you.

Gwendolen: Yes, but you don't say it.

Jack: Will you marry me, Gwendolen? (*Goes down on his knees*)

Gwendolen: Of course I will, darling. How long have you been about it! I am afraid you have had very little experience in how one should propose.

Jack: I have never loved anyone in the world but you, Gwendolen.

Gwendolen: Yes, but men often propose for practice. My brother Gerald is an example. All my girlfriends tell me so. What wonderfully blue eyes you have, Ernest! I hope you shall always look at me like that, especially in the presence of other people.

Enter **Lady Bracknell**

Lady Bracknell: Mr. Worthing! Rise, sir, from this semi-prostrate posture. It is most improper.

Gwendolen: Mamma! (*Jack tries to rise; Gwendolen restrains him*) I must request you to retire. This is no place for you. Besides, Mr. Worthing hasn't finished yet.

Lady Bracknell: Finished what, if I may ask?

Gwendolen: I am engaged to Mr. Worthing, mamma. (*They rise together*)

Lady Bracknell: You are not engaged to anyone. When you do become engaged to someone, I, or your father, his health permitting, will inform you of the same. An engagement is supposed to come to a young girl as a surprise, pleasant or unpleasant, as the case might be. An engagement is not a matter for a young girl to arrange for herself. Mr. Worthing, I have a few questions to put to you. While I do so, Gwendolen shall wait for me below in the carriage.

Gwendolen (*reproachfully*): Mamma!

Lady Bracknell: In the carriage, Gwendolen!

Gwendolen *goes to the door. She and* **Jack** *blow kisses to each other behind* **Lady Bracknell's** *back.* **Lady Bracknell** *looks about surprised as if she could not understand what the sound was. She finally turns around.*

Gwendolen, the carriage!

Gwendolen: Yes, mamma. (Exits, looking back at **Jack**.)

Lady Bracknell (Sitting down): You may take a seat, Mr. Worthing.

Looks in her pocket for notebook and pencil.

Jack: Thank you, Lady Bracknell, I prefer standing.

Lady Bracknell (*pencil and notebook in hand*): I feel bound to tell you that you are not on my list of eligible young men, although I possess the same list as the dear Duchess of Bolton does. We work together, actually. But, I am quite ready to enter your name, should your answers be what a really affectionate mother chooses to hear. Do you smoke?

Jack: Well, yes, I must admit I smoke.

Lady Bracknell: I am glad to hear that. A man must have an occupation of some kind. As it is there are far too many idle men in London. How old are you?

Jack: Twenty-nine.

Lady Bracknell: A very good age to get married at. I have always thought that a man who wishes to get married should either know everything or nothing. Which do you know?

Jack: (*After some hesitation*): I know nothing, Lady Bracknell.

Lady Bracknell: I am pleased to hear it as

I do not approve of anything that tampers with natural ignorance. You see, ignorance is like a fruit that is exotic and delicate; touch it and the bloom disappears. The whole theory of modern education is radically unsound. Fortunately, education in England produces no effect whatsoever. If it did, it would be a serious threat to the upper classes, and probably lead to acts of violence in Grosvenor Square. What is your income?

Jack: Between seven and eight thousand a year.

Lady Bracknell: In land, or in investments?

Jack: In investments, mainly.

Lady Bracknell: That is satisfactory. Between duties expected from someone in a lifetime, and duties enacted from one after death, land has stopped being either a profit or a pleasure. Land gives one position, but prevents one from maintaining that position. That's all that can be said about land.

Jack: I have a country house with some land,

however. It is about fifteen hundred acres I believe, but I don't rely upon it for my real income. In fact, I think the poachers are the only ones who make any profit out of it.

Lady Bracknell: A country house? How many bedrooms? Well, that point can be cleared up later. I hope you have a town house as well. A girl like Gwendolen could hardly be expected to live in the country.

Jack: I do own a house in Belgrave Square, but it is let by the year to Lady Bloxham. However, I can get it back anytime I want to, at six months' notice.

Lady Bracknell: I don't know Lady Bloxham.

Jack: Oh, she's an old lady who goes about very little.

Lady Bracknell: Nowadays, there is no guarantee about respectability of character. What number in Belgrave Square?

Jack: 149.

Lady Bracknell (*with a shake of her head*): The

ACT ONE

unfashionable side. However, that can easily be altered.

Jack: The fashion, or the side?

Lady Bracknell (*sternly*): Both if necessary. What about your politics?

Jack: I'm afraid I have none. I'm a Liberal Unionist.

Lady Bracknell: They count as Tories. They dine with us sometimes. Now, to minor matters. What about your parents?

Jack: I have lost both my parents.

Lady Bracknell: Both? That appears to be carelessness. Who was your father? He was obviously a man of wealth. Was he a man of commerce or did he rise from aristocracy?

Jack: I'm afraid I don't really know. I think, Lady Bracknell, it is fairer to state that my parents had lost me instead of the other way around. I do not know…who I am by birth. The truth is…I was found.

Lady Bracknell: Found!

61

Jack: The late Mr. Thomas Cardew, a kind, old gentleman found me and gave me the name of Worthing, because he happened to have a first-class ticket to Worthing in his pocket when he found me. Worthing is a seaside resort in Sussex.

Lady Bracknell: Where did this gentleman find you?

Jack (*gravely*): In a handbag.

Lady Bracknell: A handbag?

Jack (*very seriously*): Yes, Lady Bracknell. I was in a large, black leather handbag. It was an ordinary handbag with handles.

Lady Bracknell: Where did this gentleman come across this ordinary handbag?

Jack: In the cloakroom at Victoria Station. It was mistakenly given to him for his own.

Lady Bracknell: The cloakroom at Victoria Station?

Jack: Yes. The Brighton line.

Lady Bracknell: The line is inconsequential. Mr. Worthing, I must admit that I am rather

bewildered by your narrative. To be born in a handbag seems to me to be totally contemptuous for the normal decencies of family life. Why, it reminds me of the worst excesses of the French Revolution. I assume you are aware of the consequences of that unfortunate movement. Regarding the particular locality where the handbag was discovered, a railway station cloakroom serves to hide a social indiscretion. It is not the first time it has been used to do so, probably. But it does not indicate to be an assured basis for a recognised position in society.

Jack: May I ask you to advise me what to do then? I would do everything in my power to ensure Gwendolen's happiness.

Lady Bracknell: Mr. Worthing, I would strongly advise you to try and acquire some relations as soon as possible. You must make a conscious effort of producing at least one parent, of either sex, before the end of the season.

Jack: I really don't see how I can manage to do

that. But I can produce the handbag anytime, as it is in my dressing room at home. I think that should satisfy you, Mrs. Bracknell.

Lady Bracknell: Me? What has it got to do with me? Can you imagine that Lord Bracknell and I would allow our only daughter to marry into a cloakroom, and form an alliance with a parcel? Good morning, Mr. Worthing!

Lady Bracknell *sweeps out in majestic indignation.*

Jack: Good morning! (**Algernon**, *from the other room, strikes up the Wedding March.* **Jack** *looks absolutely furious, and approaches the door*) For goodness' sake, stop playing that beastly tune, Algy! You are so idiotic!

The music stops and **Algernon** *enters cheerily*

Algernon: That didn't go off all right, old boy? You don't say Gwendolen refused you? It is a way she has, always refusing people. I think it is most ill-natured of her.

Jack: No! Gwendolen is as right as a trivet. We are engaged as far as she is concerned. It is her mother who is absolutely unbearable. I've never met such a Gorgon. Well, I don't know what a Gorgon is like to be honest, but I am sure Lady Bracknell is one. But she is a monster without being a myth, which is really unfair. I beg your pardon, Algy. I really shouldn't be talking about your aunt in such a manner before you.

Algernon: I love hearing my relations abused, dear boy. It is the only thing that helps me tolerate them. Relations are simply tedious, who haven't the slightest knowledge of how to live, nor the smallest instinct when to die.

Jack: Nonsense!

Algernon: It isn't!

Jack: I don't want to argue. You always want to argue about things.

Algernon: That is precisely what things are made for.

Jack: I'd shoot myself if I thought that. Algy, do you think there is a chance of Gwendolen becoming like her mother, say in about a hundred and fifty years?

Algernon: All women become like their mothers. That is their tragedy! No man does. That's his.

Jack: Is that clever?

Algernon: It's perfectly phrased! It's as true as any observation in civilised life.

Jack: I am sick to death of cleverness. Everyone is clever nowadays. Anywhere you go, you cannot escape meeting clever people. It has become a public nuisance. I do wish we had a few fools left.

Algernon: We have.

Jack: I would like to meet them. What do they talk about?

Algernon: The clever people, of course.

Jack: What fools!

Algernon: Did you tell Gwendolen about your being Ernest in town and Jack in the country?

Jack (*patronisingly*): My dear fellow, the truth is not always told to a nice, sweet, refined girl. You have rather extraordinary ideas as to how one should behave with a woman!

Algernon: The only way to behave with a woman is to make love to her if she's pretty, and to someone else, if she's plain.

Jack: Oh, that is nonsense.

Algernon: What about your brother Ernest?

Jack: I shall get rid of him before the end of the week. I'll say he died of apoplexy in Paris. Lots of people do, don't they?

Algernon: Yes, but it's hereditary, my dear fellow. A severe chill might be better to say.

Jack: You sure a severe chill isn't hereditary?

Algernon: Of course not!

Jack: Very well then. That will get rid of him.

Algernon: But I thought Miss Cardew was a little too much interested in Ernest. Won't she feel his loss a lot?

Jack: That's all right! Cecily is not a silly romantic girl. She possesses a capital appetite,

goes for long walks, and pays no attention to her lessons.

Algernon: I would like to see Cecily.

Jack: I shall ensure you never do. She is excessively pretty, and only eighteen.

Algernon: Does Gwendolen know that you have a pretty, eighteen-year-old ward?

Jack: Oh! One does not blurt out such things to people. I am sure Cecily and Gwendolen will be great friends half an hour after they have met. They will be calling each other sister.

Algernon: Women only tend to do that after they have called each other a lot of other things first. But we must go and dress now if we hope to get a good table at Willis's. It is nearly seven. I'm hungry!

Jack: I never knew you when you weren't.

Algernon: What shall we do after dinner? Go to a theatre?

Jack: No, I loathe listening.

Algernon: The Club?

Jack: I hate talking.

Algernon: We might trot around to the Empire at ten?

Jack: No! I can't bear to look at things. It's silly!

Algernon: What shall we do then?

Jack: Nothing!

Algernon: It's awfully hard work to do nothing. I don't mind hard work if there is no definite object at hand.

Enter **Lane**.

Lane: Miss Fairfax.

Enter **Gwendolen**. *Exit* **Lane**.

Algernon: Gwendolen, upon my word!

Gwendolen: Kindly turn your back, Algy. I have something particular to say to Mr. Worthing.

Algernon: Really, Gwendolen, I don't think I can allow this.

Gwendolen: Algy, you always adopt a strictly immoral attitude towards life. You aren't old enough to do that. (**Algernon** *retires to the fireplace.*)

Jack: My own darling!

Gwendolen: Ernest, we may never be married from the expression I see on mamma's face. Few parents nowadays have any regard for the wishes of their children. The old-fashioned respect for the young is fading away quickly. I lost whatever influence I had on mamma when I was three years old. But although she might prevent our marriage, and I may marry someone else, and marry often, she can never change my eternal devotion to you.

Jack: Oh, dear Gwendolen!

Gwendolen: The story of your romantic origin, narrated with unpleasing comments by mamma, has stirred the deepest fibres of my nature. I am irresistibly fascinated by your Christian name and the simplicity of your character. I have your town address at the Albany. What is your country address?

Jack: The Manor House, Woolton, Hertfordshire.

Algernon, *who has been listening carefully, smiles to himself, and writes the address on his shirt-cuff. He then picks up the Railway Guide.*

Gwendolen: There is a good postal service, I hope? Doing something desperate might be necessary. That would require serious consideration, of course. I shall communicate with you daily.

Jack: My own one!

Gwendolen: How long will you remain in town?

Jack: Till Monday.

Gwendolen: Good! You may turn around now, Algy.

Algernon: Thanks, I've turned around already.

Gwendolen: You may also ring the bell.

Jack: Will you allow me to see you to your carriage, my darling?

Gwendolen: Certainly.

Jack (*To* **Lane**, *who now enters*): I will see Miss Fairfax out.

Lane: Yes, sir.

Jack and **Gwendolen** *go off.*

Lane *presents several letters on a salver to* **Algernon**. *It would appear that they are bills, as* **Algernon**, *after looking at the envelopes, tears them up.*

Algernon: A glass of sherry, Lane.

Lane: Yes, sir.

Algernon: I'm going Bunburying tomorrow, Lane.

Lane: Yes, sir.

Algernon: I shall probably not be back till Monday.

Lane: Yes, sir. (*Handing sherry.*)

Algernon: I hope tomorrow will be a fine day, Lane.

Lane: It never is, sir.

Algernon: Lane, you're a perfect pessimist.

Lane: I try my best to give satisfaction, sir.

Enter **Jack**. *Exit* **Lane**

Jack: What a sensible, intellectual girl! The only girl I've ever loved. (**Algernon** *is laughing away*.) What on earth amuses you so?

Algernon: Oh, I'm just anxious about poor Bunbury.

Jack: If you don't take care, your friend Bunbury will land you in a serious scrape one day.

Algernon: I love scrapes as they are the only things that are never serious.

Jack: That's nonsense, Algy. You never talk anything but nonsense.

Algernon: Nobody ever does.

Jack looks indignantly at him and leaves the room. **Algernon** lights a cigarette, reads his shirt-cuff, and smiles.

Act Two

Scene: *Time of the year: July. Garden at the Manor House, Woolton. A flight of grey stone steps leads up to the house. The garden is an old-fashioned one and is full of roses. Basket chairs and a table covered with books are set under a large yew tree.*

Miss Prism *is seen seated at the table.* **Cecily** *is at the back, watering the flowers.*

Miss Prism (*calling*): Cecily, Cecily! Surely an occupation such as the watering of flowers in the garden is more of Moulton's duty than yours? That too particularly at a moment when intellectual pleasures wait to greet you. Your German grammar is on the table, Cecily. Pray open it at page fifteen so that we can repeat yesterday's

lesson. Come here this moment, Cecily!

Cecily (*walking over very slowly*): But I don't like German. It isn't a becoming language at all. I know that I look quite plain after my German lesson.

Miss Prism: Child, you are aware how anxious your guardian is that you improve yourself in every way. He laid stress particularly on your German when he left for town yesterday. He always lays stress on your German when he leaves town.

Cecily: Dear Uncle Jack is so very serious! Sometimes he is so serious that I think he might be unwell.

Miss Prism (*drawing herself up*): Your guardian is in the best of health, and his gravity of demeanour is commendable in one so young. I'm aware of no one else possessing such a strong sense of duty and responsibility.

Cecily: I suppose that is why he looks bored when the three of us are together.

Miss Prism: Cecily! I'm surprised at you. Mr. Worthing has many troubles in his life and idle merriment and triviality have no place in his conversation. Remember his constant anxiety about his unfortunate younger brother.

Cecily: I do wish Uncle Jack would allow his unfortunate brother to visit us sometimes. We might have a good influence over him, Miss Prism. I am sure you would as you know German and geology. Those kind of things influence a man very much.

Cecily *begins to write in her diary.*

Miss Prism: (*shaking her head*): I do not think that I could produce any effect on a person that according to his own brother is weak and lazy. I have no desire to reclaim such a man. I am also not in favour of this modern mania for turning bad people into good people at a moment's notice. Let a man reap as he sows! Put away your diary, Cecily. I really don't see why you should be keeping a diary at all.

Cecily: I keep a diary to enter the wonderful secrets of my life. I shall probably forget about them if I don't write them down.

Miss Prism: Memory, my dear Cecily, is the diary that all of us carry about with us.

Cecily: Yes, but it usually chronicles the things that have never happened, and could have possibly never happened. Memory, I believe, is responsible for almost all the three-volume novels that Mudie sends us.

Miss Prism: Do not slight the three-volume novel, Cecily. Why, I wrote one myself in my earlier days.

Cecily: Did you really, Miss Prism? You are so wonderfully clever! I hope it didn't end happily. I don't like novels that end happily as they are depressing.

Miss Prism: The good ended happily, and the bad unhappily. That's what Fiction means.

Cecily: But it's unfair. Was your novel ever published?

Miss Prism: Alas! No. The manuscript was abandoned unfortunately. (**Cecily** *starts*.) I use the word meaning lost or mislaid. To work now, child, these speculations are useless.

Cecily (*smiling*): But I see Dr. Chasuble approaching through the garden.

Miss Prism (*rising and advancing*): Dr. Chasuble! A pleasure, indeed.

Enter **Canon Chasuble**.

Chasuble: And how are we this morning? I trust you are well, Miss Prism?

Cecily: Miss Prism was just complaining of a slight headache. I think a short stroll in the park with you would do her good, Dr. Chasuble.

Miss Prism: But I haven't mentioned anything about a headache, Cecily.

Cecily: No, Miss Prism. But I instinctively felt you had a headache. I was thinking about that rather than my German lesson when the Rector arrived.

Chasuble: I hope you are not inattentive, Cecily.

Cecily: I'm afraid so.

Chasuble: That's strange. If I were fortunate enough to be Miss Prism's pupil, I would hang upon her lips. (**Miss Prism** glares.) I spoke metaphorically, and my metaphor was drawn from bees. Ahem! I suppose Mr. Worthing hasn't returned from town yet?

Miss Prism: He is not expected till Monday afternoon.

Chasuble: Yes, he likes to spend his Sunday in London usually. But not for enjoyment unlike his unfortunate younger brother. But I must not disturb Egeria and her pupil any longer.

Miss Prism: Egeria? My name is Laetitia, Doctor.

Chasuble (*bowing*): Merely a classical allusion, drawn from the Pagan authors. I shall see you both at Evensong, no doubt?

Miss Prism: I think I will have a stroll with you, dear Doctor. I find I do have a headache that a walk might do good.

Chasuble: With pleasure, Miss Prism. We might go as far as the schools and back.

Miss Prism: That would be delightful. Cecily, read your Political Economy in my absence. You may omit the chapter on the 'Fall of the Rupee' as it's too sensational. Even the metallic problems have their melodramatic sides.

Goes down the garden with **Dr. Chasuble.**

Cecily (*picks up books and throws them back on the table*): Horrid Political Economy! Horrid Geography! Horrid, horrid German!

Enter **Merriman** *with a card on a salver.*

Merriman: Mr. Ernest Worthing has just driven over from the station with his luggage.

Cecily (*takes the card and reads it*): "Mr. Ernest Worthing, B.4, The Albany, W." Uncle Jack's brother! Did you tell him Mr. Worthing is in town?

Merriman: Yes, Miss. He seemed much disappointed. He said he wished to speak to you for a moment when I mentioned that you and Miss Prism were in the garden.

Cecily: Ask him to come here. I suppose you had better talk to the housekeeper about a room for him.

Merriman: Yes, Miss.

Merriman *exits.*

Cecily: I have never met a wicked person before and feel rather frightened. I am so scared that he will look just like everyone else.

Enter **Algernon**, *very gay and debonair.*

He does!

Algernon: (*raising his hat*): You are my little cousin Cecily, I'm sure.

Cecily: You are under some strange mistake. I am not little, but unusually tall for my age. (**Algernon** *is rather taken aback.*) But I am your cousin Cecily. From your card, I see that you are Uncle Jack's brother, my cousin Ernest, my wicked cousin Ernest.

Algernon: Oh! I am not wicked at all, cousin Cecily. You mustn't think that I'm wicked!

Cecily: Well, if you are not, then you are

certainly deceiving us all in a manner that's inexcusable, pretending to be wicked and being good. That's hypocrisy.

Algernon (*stares at her in amazement*): Oh! I have been really reckless!

Cecily: I am glad to hear that.

Algernon: I have been very bad in my own small way.

Cecily: Although it's not something to be proud of, I'm sure it must have been pleasant.

Algernon: Your company is much more pleasant.

Cecily: But I fail to understand you being here as Uncle Jack won't be back till Monday afternoon.

Algernon: That is a great disappointment. I have to leave by the first train on Monday morning as I have a business appointment in London that I cannot miss.

Cecily: I think you should wait for Uncle Jack. He wants to speak to you about your emigration.

Algernon: About what?

Cecily: Uncle Jack is sending you to Australia.

Algernon: Australia? I'd rather die.

Cecily: Well, he said at dinner on Wednesday night that it would be a choice between this world, the next world, and Australia.

Algernon: The accounts I have received of the next world and Australia are not very encouraging. This world is good enough for me, cousin Cecily.

Cecily: But are you good enough for it?

Algernon: I'm afraid not. That is why I wish you to reform me, if you don't mind making that your mission, cousin Cecily.

Cecily: I'm afraid I'm hard pressed for time this afternoon.

Algernon: Would you mind my reforming myself this afternoon?

Cecily: That's rather Quixotic of you. But I think you should try.

Algernon: I will. I feel better already.

Cecily: You look worse.

Algernon: That's because I'm hungry.

Cecily: How thoughtless of me! Won't you come in?

Algernon: Thank you. May I have a buttonhole first? I never develop an appetite unless I have a buttonhole first.

Cecily: A Marechal Niel? (*Picks up scissors.*)

Algernon: I'd rather have a pink rose.

Cecily: Why? (*Cuts a flower.*)

Algernon: Because you are like a pink rose, cousin Cecily.

Cecily: I don't think it is right for you to talk to me like that. Miss Prism never says such things to me.

Algernon: Then, Miss Prism is a short-sighted old lady. (*Cecily puts the rose in his buttonhole.*) You are the prettiest girl I ever saw.

Cecily: Miss Prism says all good looks are a snare.

Algernon: Every sensible man would like to be trapped in such a snare.

Cecily: Oh, I don't think I'd like to snare a sensible man. I wouldn't know what to talk to him about.

They enter the house. **Miss Prism** *and* **Dr. Chasuble** *return.*

Miss Prism: You should get married, dear Dr. Chasuble, instead of living alone. I can understand being a misanthrope, but a womanthrope, never!

Chasuble (*with a scholarly shudder*): I do not deserve such a neologistic phrase. Both the precept and the practice of the Primitive Church was specifically against matrimony.

Miss Prism: That is precisely the reason for the decline of the Primitive Church. Dear Doctor, you do not seem to realise that by persistently remaining single, a man converts himself to a permanent public temptation. Men should be careful as it is this celibacy that leads weaker vessels astray.

Chasuble: Isn't a man equally attractive when married?

Miss Prism: No married man is ever attractive except to his own wife.

Chasuble: Often, I've been told, not even to her.

Miss Prism: That depends on the intellectual sympathies of the woman. Maturity can always be depended on and ripeness, always trusted. Young women are green. (**Chasuble** *starts.*) I spoke on horticultural terms, and my metaphor was drawn from fruit. But where is Cecily?

Chasuble: Maybe she followed us to the schools.

Enter **Jack** *slowly from the back of the garden, dressed in the deepest mourning.*

Miss Prism: Mr. Worthing!

Chasuble: Mr. Worthing?

Miss Prism: What a surprise! We did not expect you till Monday afternoon.

Jack (*Shakes* **Miss Prism's** *hand in a tragic manner*): I have returned earlier than I had expected. Dr. Chasuble, I hope you are well?

Chasuble: Dear Mr. Worthing, I hope this garb of grief does not indicate some terrible calamity?

Jack: My brother.

Miss Prism: More extravagance and shameful debts?

Chasuble: Still leading his life of pleasure?

Jack (*Shaking his head*): Dead!

Chasuble: Your brother Ernest, dead?

Jack: Quite dead.

Miss Prism: What a lesson for him. I trust he will profit from it.

Chasuble: I offer you my sincerest condolence, Mr. Worthing. At least you have the consolation of knowing that you were always the most generous and forgiving of brothers.

Jack: Poor Ernest! He had many faults, but this is a very sad blow.

Chasuble: Very sad indeed! Were you with him at the end?

Jack: No, he died abroad in Paris. I received a telegram last night from the manager of the

Grand Hotel.

Chasuble: Was the cause of death mentioned?

Jack: A severe chill.

Miss Prism: A man shall reap as he sows.

Chasuble (*Raising his hand*): Charity, dear Miss Prism, charity! None of us is perfect. Will the interment take place here?

Jack: No. He expressed a desire to be buried in Paris.

Chasuble: In Paris? (*Shakes his head.*) I fear that does not indicate a serious state of mind. Undoubtedly, you would wish me to make some slight allusion to this domestic tragedy next Sunday. (**Jack** *presses his hand convulsively.*) My sermon can be adapted to any occasion, joyful or distressing as in this case. I have preached it at harvest celebrations, confirmations, christenings, on days of humiliation and festal days. The last time, my sermon was delivered in the Cathedral. The Bishop was present and struck some of my analogies.

Jack: Ah! You mentioned christenings? I suppose you know how to christen, Dr. Chasuble? (**Dr. Chasuble** *looks stunned*) I mean, you are continuously christening, aren't you?

Miss Prism: It is one of the Rector's constant duties in this parish.

Chasuble: Is there any particular infant in whom you are interested, Mr. Worthing? Your brother was unmarried, was he not?

Jack: Oh, yes.

Miss Prism (*Bitterly*): People who live entirely for pleasure normally are.

Jack: It is not for any child, dear Doctor. I would like to be christened myself, this afternoon, if you have nothing better to do.

Chasuble: But Mr. Worthing, surely you have been christened already?

Jack: I don't remember anything about it.

Chasuble: Do you have any doubts about it?

Jack: Yes. I don't know if it would bother you in any way though, or if I'm a little old for it now.

Chasuble: Not at all. The sprinkling and immersion of adults is a perfectly canonical practice.

Jack: Immersion!

Chasuble: You need not worry. Sprinkling is all that is necessary as well as advisable. Our weather is so changeable. At what hour do you wish to have the ceremony performed?

Jack: I might trot around five if it suits you.

Chasuble: Perfectly! In fact, I shall be performing two similar ceremonies around that time. Twins of Jenkins the Carter.

Jack: Oh! There's no fun in being christened along with other babies. Half-past five then?

Chasuble: Admirably! (*Consults watch.*) Now, I will no longer intrude in a house of sorrow, dear Mr. Worthing. I would beg you not to be bowed down by grief. Bitter trials are often blessings in disguise.

Miss Prism: This seems to me to be a blessing that's very obvious.

*Enter **Cecily** from the house.*

Cecily: Uncle Jack! I am pleased to see you back. But what horrid clothes you have got on! Please change them.

Miss Prism: Cecily!

Chasuble: My child!

Cecily *approaches* **Jack** *who kisses her brow in a melancholy manner.*

Cecily: What's the matter Uncle Jack? You look like you've got toothache. I've got a surprise for you that will make you happy. Who so you think is in the dining room? Your brother!

Jack: Who??

Cecily: Your brother Ernest. He arrived about half an hour ago.

Jack: What nonsense! I haven't got a brother.

Cecily: Oh, don't say that. He might have behaved badly with you in the past, but he is still your brother. How can you be so heartless as to disown him? I'll ask him to come out, and you shall shake hands with him, won't you Uncle Jack? (*Runs back into the house*)

Chasuble: These are happy tidings indeed.

Miss Prism: When we are all resigned to his loss, his sudden return does seem particularly distressing to me.

Jack: My brother is in the dining room? I don't know what this means. I think it's perfectly absurd.

Enter **Algernon** *and* **Cecily** *hand in hand. They approach* **Jack** *slowly.*

Jack: Good heavens! (*Motions* **Algernon** *away.*)

Algernon: Brother John, I have come to tell you that I'm very sorry for all the trouble I have caused you, and that I intend to lead a better life in the days to come. (**Jack** *glares at him and does not take his hand.*)

Cecily: Are you going to refuse your own brother's hand, Uncle Jack?

Jack: Nothing can make me take his hand. I think his coming here is disgraceful and he knows why.

Cecily: Be nice, Uncle Jack. There is some good in everyone. Ernest has been telling me about his poor invalid friend Mr. Bunbury whom he

visits often. There must be much good in a man who is kind to an invalid and who leaves the comforts of London to sit by a bed of pain.

Jack: He's been talking about Bunbury, has he?

Cecily: Yes.

Jack: I won't have him talk to you about Bunbury or anything else. It is enough to drive one totally frantic.

Algernon: I admit that the faults were entirely my own. But Brother John's coldness to me is what is particularly painful. I expected a warmer welcome, considering that it's the first time I've visited here.

Cecily: Uncle Jack, I shall never forgive you if you don't shake hands with Ernest.

Jack: Never forgive me?

Cecily: Never, never, never!

Jack: Well, this is the last time I'll ever do it. (*Shakes hands with* **Algernon** *and glares*.)

Chasuble: It is pleasant to witness such a perfect reconciliation. We might leave the brothers together.

Miss Prism: Cecily, come with us.

Cecily: Certainly, Miss Prism. My little task of reconciliation is done.

Chasuble: You have performed a beautiful action today, my dear child.

Miss Prism: We must not be premature in our judgments.

Cecily: I am so happy.

All of them exit except **Jack** *and* **Algernon.**

Jack: Algy, you scoundrel, you must get out of here as soon as possible. I will not allow any Bunburying here.

Enter **Merriman**

Merriman: I have put Mr. Ernest's things in the room next to yours, sir. I suppose that's all right.

Jack: What?

Merriman: Mr. Ernest's luggage, sir.

Jack: His luggage?

Merriman: Yes, sir. Three portmanteaus, a dressing case, two hat-boxes and a large luncheon-basket.

Algernon: I'm afraid I cannot stay for more than a week.

Jack: Merriman, order the dog-cart at once. Mr. Ernest has been recalled to town suddenly.

Merriman: Yes sir. (*Returns to house.*)

Algernon: What a frightful liar you are, Jack. I have not been summoned to town at all.

Jack: Yes, you have.

Algernon: Well, I haven't heard anyone call me yet.

Jack: Your duty as a gentleman calls you back.

Algernon: My duty as a gentleman has never ever interfered with my pleasures in the smallest way.

Jack: I can understand that perfectly.

Algernon: Cecily is a darling!

Jack: You are not supposed to speak of Miss Cardew like that. I do not like it.

Algernon: Well, I don't like your clothes. You look ridiculous. Why don't you go upstairs and change? It is childish to mourn for a man who

is residing with you as your guest for an entire week. Grotesque is the word!

Jack: You are NOT staying with me for an entire week as a guest or anything else. You have to leave by the four-five train.

Algernon: I refuse to leave if you are in a state of mourning. It would be most unfriendly on my part. You would stay with me if I were in mourning. I think it would be unkind if I didn't.

Jack: Will you leave if I go and change my clothes?

Algernon: Yes, if you don't take too long. I never saw anyone take so long to dress, and with such little result.

Jack: It's better than being overdressed like you.

Algernon: If I am occasionally overdressed, I make up for it by being overeducated.

Jack: Your vanity is ridiculous, your behaviour an outrage, and your presence absurd. I hope you have a pleasant journey back to town by the four-five. This Bunburying has been a failure for you this time. (*Enters the house.*)

Algernon: I think it's a great success. I'm in love with Cecily, and that is everything.

*Enter **Cecily** at the back of the garden. She begins watering the flowers with a can.*

But I must see her again before I leave. Ah, there she is!

Cecily: I came back to water the roses. I thought you were with Uncle Jack.

Algernon: He's gone to order the dog-cart for me.

Cecily: Oh, is he taking you for a nice drive?

Algernon: He's sending me away.

Cecily: Then we have to part?

Algernon: I'm afraid so. It's a very painful parting.

Cecily: It's always painful to part from someone one has known very briefly. One can endure the absence of old friends. But even a momentary separation from someone one has been just introduced to is unbearable.

Algernon: Thank you.

Enter **Merriman**

Merriman: The dog-cart is at the door, sir.

Algernon looks *appealingly* at **Cecily**

Cecily: It can wait for five minutes, Merriman.

Merriman: Yes, miss.

Exit **Merriman**

Algernon: I hope I shall not offend you, Cecily, if I tell you frankly and openly that you are the visible personification of absolute perfection to me.

Cecily: Your frankness does you great credit, Ernest. If you permit me, I shall copy your remarks into my diary. (*Goes over to table and begins writing in diary.*)

Algernon: You keep a diary? I'd give anything to have a look at it. May I?

Cecily: Oh no! (*Puts her hand over her diary.*) It's just a young girl's record of her own thoughts and impressions, and meant for publication in

the future. I hope you will order a copy when it is published. But pray, Ernest, don't stop. I love taking down from dictation. I have reached "absolute perfection." Go on. I am ready for more.

Algernon (*taken aback*): Ahem! Ahem!

Cecily: Oh, don't cough Ernest. One should speak fluently while dictating and not cough. Besides, I do not know how to spell a cough. (*Writes as* **Algernon** *speaks.*)

Algernon: (*speaking rapidly*): Cecily, ever since I gazed upon your wonderful and unparalleled beauty, I have dared to love you wildly, passionately, devotedly, hopelessly.

Cecily: Hopelessly doesn't make much sense, does it?

Algernon: Cecily!

Enter **Merriman**.

Merriman: The dog-cart awaits, sir.

Algernon: Tell it to come round next week, same time.

Merriman (*looks at* **Cecily**, *who makes no sign*): Yes, sir.

Merriman *retires*.

Cecily: Uncle Jack would be greatly annoyed if he knew you were staying on.

Algernon: I don't care about Jack. I don't care for anyone but you. I love you Cecily. Will you marry me?

Cecily: Of course, you silly boy! Why, we have been engaged for the past three months.

Algernon: We have?

Cecily: Yes, it will be exactly three months on Thursday.

Algernon: But how did we become engaged?

Cecily: Well, ever since I learnt that Uncle Jack had a younger brother who was wicked and bad, you have been the main topic of conversation between me and Miss Prism. A man who is much talked about is always rather attractive, and one does feel that there's something in him. I must admit it was foolish on my part, but I fell in love with you, Ernest.

Algernon: Darling, when was the engagement settled?

Cecily: On the 14th of February last. Tired of your ignorance about my existence, I accepted you under this dear old tree here after a lot of struggle with myself. The next day I bought this little ring in your name, and this is the little bangle with the true lover's knot I promised you always to wear.

Algernon: Did I give you this? It's very pretty, isn't it?

Cecily: Yes, you have wonderfully good taste, Ernest. It's the excuse I've always given for you leading such a bad life. Here is the box where I keep all your letters. (*Kneels at table, opens box, and produces letters tied up with blue ribbon.*)

Algernon: But dearest Cecily, I have never written you any letters.

Cecily: You need not remind me of that Ernest. I was forced to write your letters for you three times a week, and sometimes more often.

Algernon: Oh, do let me read them, Cecily.

Cecily: I couldn't possibly. That would make you far too vain. (*Replaces box.*) The three you wrote after I'd broken off the engagement are so beautiful that even I cannot read them without tears.

Algernon: But was our engagement broken off ever?

Cecily: Of course it was. On the 22nd of last March. See my entry. (*Shows diary.*) "Today I broke off my engagement with Ernest. I feel it's better to do so. The weather continues to be charming."

Algernon: But why on earth did you break it off? What had I done? Nothing at all! I am very hurt indeed to hear that you broke it off. Especially as the weather had been charming.

Cecily: Well, it would have hardly been a serious engagement if it hadn't been broken off at least once. I forgave you before the week was out.

Algernon (*Kneeling before her*): What a perfect angel you are, Cecily.

Cecily: You dear, romantic boy. (*He kisses her, she runs her fingers through his hair.*) I hope your hair curls naturally?

Algernon: Yes darling, with a little help from others.

Cecily: I am so happy.

Algernon: You won't break off our engagement again, will you Cecily?

Cecily: I don't think I can ever do that now that I've met you. Besides, there is the question of your name, of course.

Algernon: Yes, of course. (*Nervously.*)

Cecily: You mustn't laugh at me darling, but I have always nourished a childhood dream of loving someone who is named Ernest.

Algernon *rises and so does* **Cecily**.

Cecily: There is something in the name Ernest that seems to inspire absolute confidence. I just pity any poor married woman who does not have a husband named Ernest.

Algernon: But darling, do you mean to say that you wouldn't have loved me if I had any other name?

Cecily: But what name?

Algernon: Oh, any name you like. Algernon for instance.

Cecily: I don't like the name Algernon.

Algernon: But my sweet darling, I can see no reason why you should object to a name like Algernon. It is not a bad name at all. On the contrary, it is a rather aristocratic name. Did you know that half of the chaps who get into the Bankruptcy Court go by the name of Algernon? Seriously Cecily, (*advancing towards her*) had my name been Algy, wouldn't you have loved me?

Cecily: (*rising*): I might respect you, Ernest, and I might admire your character, but I fear that I would be unable to give you my undivided attention.

Algernon: Ahem! Cecily! (*Picking up his hat.*) I

suppose your Rector here is totally experienced in the practice of all the rites and ceremonials of the Church?

Cecily: Oh, yes. Dr. Chasuble is a most learned man. He has not written a single book, so you can imagine how much he knows.

Algernon: I must see him at once on a christening that's most important- I mean on business that's most important.

Cecily: Oh!

Algernon: I shall only be away for half an hour.

Cecily: Considering the fact that we have been engaged since February the 14th, and that I met you today for the first time in my life, I think it is rather hard that you should leave me for such a long period as half an hour. Couldn't you make it twenty minutes?

Algernon: I'll be back in no time at all. (*Kisses her and rushes down the garden.*)

Cecily: What a hasty boy he is! I like his hair so much! I must enter his proposal in my diary.

Enter **Merriman**

Merriman: A Miss Fairfax has just called to see Mr. Worthing. She states that she has very important business.

Cecily: Isn't Mr. Worthing in his library?

Merriman: Mr. Worthing went over in the direction of the Rectory some time ago.

Cecily: Pray ask the lady to come out here as Mr. Worthing will be back soon surely. And you can bring tea.

Merriman: Yes, Miss. (*Exits.*)

Cecily: Miss Fairfax! I think she is one of the many elderly good women associated with Uncle Jack's philanthropic work in London. But I don't quite like women who are involved in philanthropic work. I think it's too forward of them.

Enter **Merriman**

Merriman: Miss Fairfax.

Enter **Gwendolyn**. *Exit* **Merriman**.

Cecily (*Advancing to meet her*): Let me introduce

myself. My name is Cecily Cardew.

Gwendolyn: Cecily Cardew? (*Advancing and shaking hands.*) What a sweet name! Something tells me that we are going to be very good friends. I already like you more than I can say. Let me tell you that my first impressions of people are never wrong.

Cecily: How nice of you to like me so much even though we have known each other for such a comparatively short time. Please sit down.

Gwendolyn: (*Still standing*): May I call you Cecily?

Cecily: With pleasure!

Gwendolyn: You will call me Gwendolyn, won't you?

Cecily: If you wish.

Gwendolyn: Then that is settled.

Cecily: I hope so.

A pause. They sit down together.

Gwendolyn: Allow me to introduce myself. My father is Lord Bracknell. I suppose you have never heard of papa.

Cecily: I don't think so.

Gwendolyn: I am glad to state that papa is entirely unknown outside the family circle. I think that is the way it should be. The home according to me is the proper sphere for the man. Once a man begins to neglect his domestic duties, he transforms into someone painfully effeminate, does he not? I don't like that at all. It makes men so attractive. Mama's views on education are rather strict, and she has raised me to be totally short-sighted, which is part of her system. I hope you don't mind me looking at you through my glasses?

Cecily: Oh! Not at all Gwendolyn. I am very fond of being looked at.

Gwendolyn: (*After examining* **Cecily** *carefully through a lorgnette*): You are here on a short visit, I suppose.

Cecily: Oh no! I live here.

Gwendolyn: (*severely*): Really? Undoubtedly, your mother, or some older female relative, resides here as well?

Cecily: No! I have no mother. Nor do I have any relations.

Gwendolyn: Indeed?

Cecily: My dear guardian, with Miss Prism's assistance, has the tedious task of looking after me.

Gwendolyn: Your guardian?

Cecily: Yes. I am Mr. Worthing's ward.

Gwendolyn: Really? It is strange that he never mentioned to me that he had a ward. How secretive of Mr. Worthing! He grows more interesting by the hour. I am unsure however, if this news brings me unmixed delight. (*Rising and approaching her.*) I am very fond of you Cecily, and liked you instantly when I saw you. But I am forced to state that now that I am aware that you are Mr. Worthing's ward, I do wish that you were a little older than what you are, and not so alluring in appearance. If I may speak candidly....

Cecily: Pray do! I think one should be candid whenever one has to say anything unpleasant.

Gwendolyn: Well, Cecily, I do wish that you were forty-two, and more than unusually plain for your age. Ernest has a nature that's strong and upright, and he's the very epitome of truth and honour. Being disloyal would be as impossible to him as being deceptive. But even men in possession of the noblest possible moral character have proven to be extremely susceptible to the influence of physical charms of others. Modern as well as Ancient History bears testimony about many painful examples regarding what I speak about. History, in fact, would be quite unreadable if this were not so.

Cecily: I beg your pardon, Gwendolen. Did you say Ernest?

Gwendolyn: Yes.

Cecily: But it is not Mr. Ernest Worthing who is my guardian. It is his elder brother.

Gwendolyn (*sitting down again*): Ernest never said anything about an elder brother.

Cecily: I am sorry to state that they haven't been on good terms for quite some time.

Gwendolyn: Ah, that explains it. Now that I think of it, I have never heard any man mention his elder brother. Most men seem to find this subject distasteful. You have lifted a load off my mind, Cecily. I must admit I was growing most anxious. It would have been terrible if any cloud had affected our friendship, wouldn't it? But are you quite sure that Mr. Ernest Worthing is not your guardian?

Cecily: Quite sure. In fact, I am going to be his.

Gwendolyn: I beg your pardon?

Cecily: (*rather shy and confident*): There is no reason why I should keep it a secret from you, Gwendolen. In fact, our little country newspaper is sure to publish the news next week. Mr. Ernest Worthing and I are engaged to be married.

Gwendolyn (*quite politely, rising*): Darling Cecily, there must be some slight error. The

announcement will appear in the Morning Post on Saturday at the latest. You see, Mr. Ernest Worthing is engaged to me.

Cecily: I'm afraid you must be under some strange misconception. Ernest proposed to me exactly ten minutes ago. (*Displays diary.*)

Gwendolyn (*examines diary through her lorgnette carefully*): It is certainly rather curious, as he asked me to be his wife yesterday afternoon at 5:30. Please verify the incident if you would care to do so. (*Produces her own diary.*) I never travel without my diary, you see. After all, one should have sensational reading material on a train. I am extremely sorry, dear Cecily, if this has caused you great disappointment. But I'm afraid that I have the prior claim.

Cecily: It would distress me more than anything, dear Gwendolen, if this causes you mental or physical pain. But I am bound to point out to you that since Ernest proposed to you, it is clear that

he has changed his mind about marrying you.

Gwendolyn (*meditatively*): If the poor fellow has been trapped into some foolish promise, it is my duty to rescue him instantly, and with a firm hand.

Cecily (*thoughtfully and sadly*): Whatever unfortunate entanglement my dear boy might have been led into, I shall never reproach him with it after our marriage.

Gwendolyn: Do you refer to me as an entanglement, Miss Cardew? Let me tell you that you are being presumptuous. On such an occasion it is more than a moral duty for one to speak one's mind. In fact, it becomes a pleasure.

Cecily: Are you suggesting, Miss Fairfax, that I trapped Ernest into being engaged to me? How dare you assume such a thing? I'm afraid this is hardly the time for one to put on the shallow mask of manners. I call a spade a spade when I see one.

Gwendolyn (*satirically*): I am happy to state that I have never seen a spade. It is quite apparent that our social spheres have been widely different.

Enter **Merriman**, *followed by a footman. He carries a salver, table cloth, and plate stand.* **Cecily** *is about to retort. The presence of the servants brings about a restraining influence, quietening both the girls.*

Merriman: Shall I lay tea here as usual, Miss?

Cecily (*sternly but calmly*): Yes, as usual.

Merriman *begins to clear the table. A long pause.* **Gwendolyn** *and* **Cecily** *glare at each other.*

Gwendolyn: Are there many interesting walks in the vicinity, Miss Cardew?

Cecily: Oh yes! A great many, in fact. One can see five counties from the top of one of the hills.

Gwendolyn: Five counties! I don't think I'd like that. I hate crowds.

Cecily (*sweetly*): Is that the reason why you reside in town?

Gwendolyn bites her lip, and beats her foot nervously with her parasol.

Gwendolyn (*looking around*): This is a rather well-kept garden, Miss Cardew.

Cecily: I am so glad you like it, Miss Fairfax.

Gwendolyn: Well, I had no idea that there were any flowers in the country.

Cecily: Oh, flowers are as common here as people are in London, Miss Fairfax.

Gwendolyn: If you ask me, I just fail to understand how anyone manages to exist in the country, if anybody who is actually anybody does. The country always manages to bore me to death.

Cecily: The newspapers call that agricultural depression, don't they? I think the aristocracy suffer a lot because of it presently. Why, it is almost an epidemic amongst them, I have heard. May I offer you some tea, Miss Fairfax?

Gwendolyn (*with elaborate politeness*): Thank

you. (*Aside.*) Despicable girl! But I need tea!

Cecily (*sweetly*): Sugar?

Gwendolyn: No, thank you. Sugar is not fashionable any more.

    Cecily *stares at her angrily, takes up the tongs and puts four lumps of sugar into the cup.*

Cecily (*severely*): Cake or bread or butter?

Gwendolyn (*in a bored manner*): Bread and butter, please. Cake is something that's rarely seen at the best houses these days.

Cecily (*cuts a very large slice of cake and places it on the tray*): Hand it to Miss Fairfax.

    Merriman *does so, and exits with the footman.*

Gwendolyn *drinks the tea and grimaces. She puts down the cup at once, and reaches out for the bread and butter, only to discover that it is cake. Rises in anger.*

Gwendolyn: You have filled my tea with lumps of sugar, and although I clearly asked for bread and butter, you have served me cake. I am well known for my gentleness and the extraordinary sweetness of my nature, but I warn you Miss Cardew, you go too far.

Cecily (*rising*): To save my poor, innocent, trusting boy from the schemes of any other girl there are no lengths to which I would not go.

Gwendolyn: I distrusted you from the very moment I saw you. I knew you were false and deceitful. Let me tell you that I am never deceived in such matters. My first impressions of people are always right.

Cecily: It appears that I am trespassing on your precious time, Miss Fairfax. Undoubtedly you have many other calls of a similar nature to make in the neighbourhood.

Enter **Jack**

Gwendolyn (*catching sight of him*): Ernest! My dear own Ernest!

Jack: Gwendolyn! Darling! (*Offers to kiss her.*)

Gwendolyn: One moment! Are you engaged to be married to this young lady? (*Points to* **Cecily**.)

Jack (*laughing*): To dear little Cecily! Of course not! Whatever put that idea into your pretty little head?

Gwendolyn: Thank you. You may. (*Offers her cheek.*)

Cecily (*very sweetly*): I knew there must be some misunderstanding, Miss Fairfax. The gentleman whose arm is presently round your waist is Mr. John Worthing, my guardian.

Gwendolyn: I beg your pardon?

Cecily: This is Uncle Jack.

Gwendolyn (*receding*): Jack! Oh!

Enter **Algernon**

Cecily: Here is Ernest!

Algernon (*goes straight to* **Cecily** *without noticing anyone else present*): My own love! (*Offers to kiss her.*)

Cecily (*drawing back*): One moment, Ernest! Are you engaged to be married to this young lady?

Algernon (*looking around*): To what young lady? Good heavens! Gwendolen!

Cecily: Yes! To good heavens, Gwendolen, I mean to Gwendolen!

Algernon (*laughing*): Of course not! What put such an idea into your pretty little head?

Cecily: Thank you. (Presenting her cheek to be kissed.) You may.

(**Algernon** *kisses her*)

Gwendolyn: I knew there was a slight error, Miss Cardew. The gentleman who is now embracing you is my cousin, Mr. Algernon Moncrieff.

Cecily (*breaking away from* **Algernon**): Oh! Algernon Moncrieff!

The two girls move towards each other and put their arms round each other's waists as if for protection.

Cecily: Are you called Algernon?

Algernon: I cannot deny that.

Cecily: Oh!

Gwendolyn: Is your name really John?

Jack (*proudly*): I could deny it. But my name certainly is John. It has been John for years.

Cecily (*to* **Gwendolyn**): Then both of us have been victims of a gross deception.

Gwendolyn: My sweet wronged Cecily!

Cecily: My poor wounded Gwendolen!

Gwendolyn (*slowly and seriously*): You will call me sister, won't you?

They embrace. **Jack** *and* **Algernon** *groan and pace up and down.*

Cecily: I would like to ask my guardian just one question.

Gwendolyn: An excellent idea! Mr. Worthing, I would like to ask you just one question. Where is your brother Ernest? We are both engaged to be married to your brother Ernest, so it is of utmost importance to us to know where your brother Ernest is presently.

Jack (*slowly and hesitatingly*): Gwendolen, Cecily, it is rather painful for me to be forced to speak the truth in such a way. I have been reduced to such a painful position for the first time ever in my life, and I must admit that I am

really quite inexperienced in doing anything like this. However, let me tell you both quite frankly that I have no brother called Ernest. In fact, I have no brother at all. I have never had a brother in my life, and I certainly do not have any intention of ever having a brother in the future.

Cecily (*surprised*): No brother at all?

Jack (*cheerily*): None!

Gwendolyn (*severely*): Have you never had a brother of any kind?

Jack (*pleasantly*): Never. Not of any kind.

Gwendolyn: Then I am afraid it is quite clear, Cecily, that neither of us is engaged to be married to anyone at all.

Cecily: It is not a very pleasant position for a young girl to suddenly find herself in, is it?

Gwendolyn: Let us enter the house. They will hardly dare to come after us there.

Cecily: No. Men are so cowardly, aren't they?

They retire into the house, casting scornful looks.

Jack: This beastly state of things is what you term as Bunburying, I suppose?

Algernon: Yes, and what a perfectly wonderful Bunbury it is! Why, it is the most wonderful Bunbury I have ever experienced in my life.

Jack: Well, let me tell you that you have no right whatsoever to Bunbury here.

Algernon: That is absurd. One has the right to Bunbury wherever one chooses to. Every serious Bunburyist knows this!

Jack: Serious Bunburyist! Good Lord!

Algernon: Well, one must be serious about something, if one wants to derive any amusement from life. I happen to be serious about Bunburying, and haven't the slightest idea as to what it is that you are serious about. About everything, I should fancy. You have such a trivial nature, after all.

Jack: Well, the only satisfaction that I have from this entire wretched business is that your friend Bunbury has totally exploded. You will never

be able to run down to the country as often as you used to earlier, my dear Algy. I think it's not a bad thing too.

Algernon: Your brother Ernest is a little off colour now, isn't he dear Jack? You won't be able to disappear to London now as frequently as you used to earlier. Your wicked custom has ended. I think it's not a bad thing too.

Jack: Your conduct towards Miss Cardew is inexcusable. To think of taking in a sweet, simple and innocent girl like that. Not to mention that she is my ward.

Algernon: There is no excuse in your deceiving a clever, brilliant and experienced lady like Miss Fairfax. Not to mention that she is my cousin.

Jack: All I wanted to was to be engaged to Gwendolen, as I loved her.

Algernon: Well, I just wanted to be engaged to Cecily, as I adore her.

Jack: There is definitely no chance of your marrying Miss Cardew.

Algernon: I don't think there's much chance of

you and Miss Fairfax being united, Jack.

Jack: Well, that is no business of yours.

Algernon: If it was my business, I wouldn't talk about it. (*Begins eating muffins*) It is rather vulgar to talk about one's business. Only people like stockbrokers do that, and mostly at dinner parties.

Jack: I cannot fathom how you can sit there, calmly eating muffins, when we are in this terrible trouble. You appear to me to be totally heartless.

Algernon: Well, I cannot possibly eat muffins in an agitated manner. The butter would probably get on my cuffs then. I think one should always eat muffins calmly as that is the only way to eat them.

Jack: I think it's heartless for you to be eating muffins considering the circumstances.

Algernon: Eating is the only thing that consoles me when I'm in trouble. When I am in great trouble, as anyone who knows me intimately

will testify, I refuse everything except food and drink. Presently, I am eating muffins because I am unhappy. Also, I'm particularly fond of muffins. (*Rising.*)

Jack (rising): But that is no reason for you to eat them so greedily. (*Takes muffins from* **Algernon**)

Algernon (*offering tea-cake*): I wish you would have tea-cake as I don't happen to like them.

Jack: Good heavens! A man would eat his own muffins in his own garden, I suppose.

Algernon: But didn't you just say that it was perfectly heartless to eat muffins?

Jack: I said it was perfectly heartless for you, under the circumstances. That is a different thing altogether.

Algernon: Perhaps! But the muffins are the same. (*Seizes the muffin dish from* **Jack**)

Jack: Algy, I wish to goodness that you would leave.

Algernon: You can't possibly ask me to leave without having dinner. It's absurd! I never leave without my dinner. No one ever does, barring

173

vegetarians and people like that, of course. Besides, I have just made arrangements with Dr. Chasuble to be christened under the name of Ernest at a quarter to six.

Jack: My dear fellow, the sooner you give up that nonsense, the better it will be for you. I have made arrangements this morning with Dr. Chasuble to be christened at 5:30 myself. Naturally, I shall be taking the name of Ernest as Gwendolen would want that very much. Now, both of us cannot be christened Ernest as that is absurd. Also, I have a perfect right to be christened if I like as there is no evidence whatsoever that I have ever been christened by anyone. Dr. Chasuble shares my view that it is extremely probable that I have never been christened. But your case is totally different as you have been christened already, my friend.

Algernon: Yes, but I haven't been christened for years.

Jack: Yes, but the important thing is that you have been christened.

Algernon: That's true. That is why I know that my constitution can stand it. If you are unsure about your being christened before, I dare say it is rather dangerous to venture into it now as it could make you very unwell. It might be in your memory as to how someone very closely connected with you was almost taken away in Paris this week by a severe chill.

Jack: Yes, but you had said yourself that a severe chill was not hereditary.

Algernon: It wasn't, I know. But I think it is now. You know how Science is always creating wonderful improvements in all things.

Jack (*picking up the muffin dish*): Oh, that is sheer nonsense. You are always speaking nonsense!

Algernon: Jack, you are attacking the muffins again. I wish you wouldn't do that as there are only two left. (*Takes the muffins*) I had mentioned to you that I'm particularly fond of muffins.

Jack: But I hate tea-cake.

Algernon: Then why on earth do you allow tea-cake to be served up for your guests? What thoughts you have for hospitality!

Jack: Algernon! I have already told you to leave. I do not want you here. Why don't you leave?

Algernon: Well, for starters, I haven't quite finished my tea yet! Then, there is still one muffin left.

Jack groans, and sinks into a chair. **Algernon** *still continues eating.*

Act Three

Scene: *Drawing room at the Manor House, Woolton.*
Gwendolen and Cecily are at the window, overlooking
the garden.

Gwendolen: They did not follow us into the house instantly, as anyone else would have done. This shows that they still have some sense of shame left.

Cecily: They have been eating muffins. That looks like repentance.

Gwendolen (*after a pause*): They don't appear to notice us at all. Can you cough to catch their attention?

Cecily: But I haven't got a cough.

Gwendolen: They are staring at us. What effrontery!

Cecily: They are approaching us. That's very forward of them.

Gwendolen: Let us maintain a dignified silence.

Cecily: Of course. That's the only thing left to do now.

Enter **Jack** *followed by* **Algernon**. *They whistle a dreadful popular air from a British Opera.*

Gwendolen: This dignified silence that we have decided to maintain is producing the most unpleasant effect.

Cecily: A most distasteful one.

Gwendolen: But we shall not speak first.

Cecily: Definitely not.

Gwendolen: Mr. Worthing, I have something rather important to ask you. A lot depends upon your reply.

Cecily: Gwendolen, your common sense is priceless. Mr. Moncrieff, kindly answer the question I have for you. Why on earth did you

pretend to be my guardian's brother?

Algernon: So that I might have an opportunity to meet you.

Cecily (to **Gwendolen**): That seems to be an explanation that is satisfactory, doesn't it?

Gwendolen: Yes, dear, if you can believe him.

Cecily: Well, the truth is that I don't. But that does not affect the wonderful beauty of his reply.

Gwendolen: True. When matters are gravely important, style is more vital than sincerity. Mr. Worthing, pray give me an explanation for pretending to have a brother by the name of Ernest? Was this because this gave you an opportunity to come to town and see me as often as possible?

Jack: Can you doubt it, Miss Fairfax?

Gwendolen: Well, even though I have the greatest doubts upon the subject, I plan to crush them. Truly, this is not the moment for German scepticism. (*Moving to Cecily*) Their explanations do seem satisfactory though,

especially Mr. Worthing's. It does appear to me to have the stamp of truth upon it.

Cecily: I am more than happy in Mr. Moncrieff's explanation. His voice alone is the testimony of complete credulity.

Gwendolen: Then you think that we should forgive them?

Cecily: Yes. I mean no.

Gwendolen: True! I had forgotten. There are certain principles at stake that one simply cannot afford to surrender. Which one of us should tell them? The task, one must admit, is not a pleasant one.

Cecily: Couldn't both of us speak simultaneously?

Gwendolen: That's an excellent idea! I always speak at the same time as other people. Will you be kind enough to take the time from me?

Cecily: Certainly.

Gwendolen beats time with uplifted finger.

Gwendolen and **Cecily** (*speaking together*): Your Christian names are still an impossible barrier.

That is all!

Jack and **Algernon** (*speaking together*): Our Christian names! Is that all? But we are going to be christened this afternoon.

Gwendolen (to **Jack**): Are you willing to do this terrible thing for my sake?

Jack: I am.

Cecily (*to* **Algernon**): Are you ready to face this fearful ordeal to please me?

Algernon: I am.

Gwendolen: How absurd it is to speak about the equality of the sexes! Where matters of self-sacrifice are concerned, men are undoubtedly infinitely beyond us.

Jack: We are. (*Clasps hands with* **Algernon**)

Cecily: They have their moments of bravery and physical courage that we women are absolutely unaware of.

Gwendolen (*to* **Jack**): Darling!

Algernon (*to* **Cecily**): Darling!

They fall into each other's arms.

Enter **Merriman**. *After entering, he coughs loudly on seeing the situation.*

Merriman: Ahem! Ahem! Lady Bracknell!

Jack: Good heavens!

Enter **Lady Bracknell**. *The couples separate in alarm. Exit* **Merriman**.

Lady Bracknell: Gwendolen! What does this mean?

Gwendolen: Merely the fact that I'm engaged to be married to Mr. Worthing, mamma.

Lady Bracknell: Come here and sit down immediately. Hesitation of any kind indicates mental decay in the young and physical weakness in the old. (*Turns to* **Jack**) Sir, I was informed of my daughter's sudden flight by her trusted maid. I purchased her confidence with a small coin, and followed my daughter instantly by a luggage train. Her father is under the impression that she is attending an unusually lengthy lecture by the University Extension Scheme on the Influence of a Permanent Income on Thought. I do not propose to tell him the

truth as I would consider it wrong. But you must understand that all further communication between you and my daughter must cease immediately, right from this very moment. On this matter, as indeed on all matters, I am firm.

Jack: Lady Bracknell, I am engaged to be married to Gwendolen.

Lady Bracknell: You are nothing of the kind, sir. Now, as for Algernon...Algernon!

Algernon: Yes, Aunt Augusta.

Lady Bracknell: May I enquire if this is the house where your invalid friend Mr. Bunbury resides?

Algernon (*stammering*): Oh...no! Bunbury doesn't live here. He is somewhere else presently. In fact, Bunbury is dead!

Lady Bracknell: Dead? When did Mr. Bunbury die? His death must have occurred suddenly.

Algernon: Well, I killed him this afternoon. I mean poor Bunbury died this afternoon.

Lady Bracknell: How did he die?

Algernon: Well, poor Bunbury sort of exploded.

Lady Bracknell: Exploded! Was he the victim of a revolutionary attack? I was not aware that Mr. Bunbury was interested in social legislation of any kind. If he was, I must say that he has been well punished for being so morbid.

Algernon: Dear Aunt Augusta, what I mean to say is that poor Bunbury was found out! The doctors discovered that Bunbury could not live any longer, and that is what I mean. Bunbury died!

Lady Bracknell: Well, all I can say is that he seems to have had great confidence in the opinion of his physicians. However, what makes me happy is that Mr. Bunbury made up his mind to embark upon a definite course of action, and acted under proper medical advice. Now that we have finally got rid of this Mr. Bunbury, may I enquire, Mr. Worthing, who is that young lady whose hand my nephew Algernon is now holding in what appears to me to be especially unnecessary?

Jack: That lady is my ward, Miss Cecily Cardew.

Lady Bracknell *bows coldly to* **Cecily**.

Algernon: Aunt Augusta, I am engaged to be married to Cecily.

Lady Bracknell: I beg your pardon, Algernon?

Cecily: Mr. Moncrief and I are engaged to be married, Lady Bracknell.

Lady Bracknell (*shivers, and crosses to the sofa to sit down*): I am unaware if there is something that is strangely exciting in the air of this particular part of Hertfordshire, but the number of engagements that take place seems to me considerably above the proper average that has been provided by statistics for our guidance. Mr. Worthing, I daresay that a little preliminary inquiry on my part would not seem to be out of place. Is Miss Cardew associated with any of the larger railway stations in London? I merely seek to obtain information. Until yesterday I was unaware that any families or people were in actual existence whose origin was a Terminus.

Jack *looks absolutely furious, but manages to restrain himself.*

Jack (*in a crystal clear, cold voice*): Miss Cardew is the granddaughter of the late Mr. Thomas Cardew of 149 Belgrave Square, S.W.; Gervase Park, Dorking, Surrey; and the Sporran, Fifeshire, N.B.

Lady Bracknell: That does not sound unsatisfactory to me. Three addresses are enough to inspire confidence, even in tradesmen. But what proof is there that they are authentic?

Jack: Well, I have carefully preserved the Court Guides of the period. They are there for your inspection, Lady Bracknell.

Lady Bracknell (*grimly*): I have known strange errors that existed in that particular publication.

Jack: Well, let me inform you that Miss Cardew's family solicitors are Messrs. Markby, Markby and Markby.

Lady Bracknell: Markby, Markby and Markby? A firm of the very highest position in their

particular profession, indeed. I am informed that one of the Mr. Markby's is seen occasionally at dinner parties. I must say that I am satisfied so far.

Jack (*in an irritated manner*): That's extremely kind of you, Lady Bracknell! You will also be rather pleased to know that I also happen to possess certificates of Miss Cardew's birth, baptism, whooping cough, registration, vaccination, confirmation, and the measles; both of the German as well as the English variety.

Lady Bracknell: Ah! A life that has been crowded with incident, I see. I think it has also been a life that is probably too exciting for a young girl. I must say that I am not personally in favour of premature experiences myself. (*Rises, and studies her watch*)

Gwendolen! It is time for our departure. We do not have a moment to lose. By the way, Mr. Worthing, as a matter of form I suppose I better ask you if Miss Cardew is in possession of any fortune?

Jack: Well, about a hundred and thirty thousand pounds in the Funds. That is all. Goodbye, Lady Bracknell. I am so pleased to have seen you.

Lady Bracknell (*sitting down again*): Just one moment, Mr. Worthing. Did you say a hundred and thirty thousand pounds? And in the Funds! Miss Cardew appears to me to be a wonderfully attractive lady, now that I look at her properly. Very few girls of the present day seem to possess any really solid qualities, any of the qualities that are everlasting, and mature with time. I regret to declare that we live in an age of surfaces. (*To* **Cecily**): Come over here, dear. (**Cecily** *goes across*) Pretty child! Your dress is sadly simple, of course, and your hair is just like Nature has chosen to leave it. But we can soon alter all of that. Nothing like the expertise of a thoroughly experienced French maid to produce the most marvelous result in a short span of time. I remember that I had recommended one to young Lady Lancing, and after three months, even her own husband did not know her.

Jack: And after six months no one knew her.

Lady Bracknell (*glares at* **Jack** for a few minutes. Then bends towards **Cecily** with a practiced smile) : Pray, turn around now, sweet child.

(**Cecily** *turns completely around.*) No, what I want is the side view, dear.

(**Cecily** *presents her profile.*) Yes, just as I had expected. There are distinct social possibilities that exist in your profile. The two weak points in our age are its want of profile and its want of principle. The chin a little higher, my dear. Style is largely dependent on the way the chin is worn. The chin is worn very high, just as present. Algernon!

Algernon: Yes, Aunt Augusta!

Lady Bracknell: Miss Cardew's profile has

distinct social possibilities.

Algernon: Cecily is the prettiest, dearest, sweetest girl in the whole world. I don't care twopence about social possibilities.

Lady Bracknell: Algernon, I would urge you to never speak disrespectfully of Society. Only people who fail to get into it, do that. (*To* **Cecily**): Dear child, of course you are aware that Algernon has nothing but his debts to depend upon. But I, for one, do not approve of mercenary marriages. I recall when I married Lord Bracknell, I did not have any fortune of any kind whatsoever. But never for a moment did I dream of allowing that to stand in my way. So, I suppose I must give my consent.

Algernon: Thank you, Aunt Augusta.

Lady Bracknell: Cecily, you may kiss me!

Cecily: (*kisses her*): Thank you, Lady Bracknell.

Lady Bracknell: You may also address me as Aunt Augusta for the future.

Cecily: Thank you, Aunt Augusta.

Lady Bracknell: I think that the marriage had better take place quite soon.

Algernon: Thank you, Aunt Augusta.

Cecily: Thank you, Aunt Augusta.

Lady Bracknell: To speak my mind frankly, I am not in favour of long engagements. They serve nothing except give people the opportunity to discover each other's character before marriage. Such a thing, I think is never advisable.

Jack: I beg your pardon for interrupting you, Lady Bracknell, but I fear that this engagement is quite out of the question. I am Miss Cardew's guardian, and she cannot marry without my consent till the time she comes of age. I am afraid I absolutely refuse to give that consent.

Lady Bracknell: May I ask upon what grounds? I must say that Algernon is an extremely, in fact ostentatiously, eligible young man. Although he has nothing, he looks everything. What more can one desire?

Jack: Lady Bracknell, it pains me a lot to have to speak so frankly to you about your nephew. But the fact is that I do not approve of his moral character at all. The truth is that I suspect him of being untruthful.

Algernon *and* **Cecily** stare at him in indignant amazement.

Lady Bracknell: Untruthful? My nephew Algernon? Why, that's impossible! He is an Oxonian.

Jack: I am afraid that there can be no doubt at all over the matter. Why, this very afternoon during my temporary absence in London on an important question of romance, Algernon obtained admission into my house by pretending to be my brother. I have just been informed by my butler that Algernon, under the assumed name of my brother, consumed an entire pint bottle of my Perrier-Jouet, Brut, '89. I had contemplated reserving this special wine for myself. Also, under the guise of this disgraceful

deception, he succeeded to alienate the affections of my only ward in the course of the afternoon. Subsequently, Algernon decided to stay over for tea, and then devoured every single muffin that existed. What makes his conduct all the more heartless is the fact that he was perfectly aware that I have no brother, never had a brother, and that I do not intend to have a brother, not even of any kind. I had conveyed the same to him myself yesterday afternoon.

Lady Bracknell: Ahem! After careful consideration, I have arrived at the decision to entirely overlook my nephew's conduct to you, Mr. Worthing.

Jack: That is very generous of you indeed, Lady Bracknell. However, my own decision cannot be reversed. I refuse to give my consent to this marriage.

Lady Bracknell (*to* **Cecily**): Come here, my sweet child. (**Cecily** *moves across to her.*) How old are you, my dear?

Cecily: Well, I am only eighteen, really. But I always admit to being twenty years old when I go to attend evening parties.

Lady Bracknell: You are absolutely right to make that slight alteration. Truly, no woman should ever be perfectly accurate about her age. It does look so calculating.... (*In a meditative manner*) Eighteen years old, but admitting to be twenty at evening parties. Well, I think it won't be very long before you are of age and free from the restraints and impositions of tutelage. Hence, I feel that your guardian's consent is not a matter of any importance, after all.

Jack: Excuse me for interrupting you again, Lady Bracknell. But I think it is only fair on my part to inform you that according to the terms of her grandfather's will, Miss Cardew does not come legally of age till she is thirty-five years old.

Lady Bracknell: That does not seem to be a serious objection at all. Thirty-five is a rather attractive age after all. London society is full of women of the very highest birth who have remained thirty-five for many years of their own free choice. Lady Dumbleton is a perfect example. As per my knowledge, she has been thirty-five ever since she arrived at the age of forty, which was many years ago now. So, I see absolutely no reason why our dear Cecily should not be as attractive at the age of thirty-five than she presently is. There will be a large accumulation of property.

Cecily: Could you wait for me till I am thirty-five, dear Algy?

Algernon: Of course! You know I could, my dear.

Cecily: Yes, I felt it instinctively. But the truth is that I couldn't wait for so long a time myself. Why, I hate waiting even five minutes for someone. It always makes me rather cross. I know that I am not a punctual person myself, but I do like punctuality in others. Waiting, even to get married is simply out of the question, I am afraid.

Algernon: Then, what do we do, Cecily?

Cecily: I am afraid I don't know, Mr. Moncrieff.

Lady Bracknell: My dear Mr. Worthing, as Miss Cecily categorically states that she cannot wait till she is thirty-five years to be married, a remark which I am forced to say suggests to me to display a nature that is somewhat impatient, may I beg you to reconsider your decision?

Jack: But my dear Lady Bracknell, the matter is totally in your own hands. The moment you give your consent to my marriage with Gwendolen, I shall most happily allow your nephew to be united in marriage with my ward.

Lady Bracknell (*rising and drawing herself up to her full height.*): You must be aware that what you are proposing is totally out of the question, sir.

Jack: Then I'm afraid a passionate celibacy is all that any of us can really look forward to.

Lady Bracknell: That is not the destiny that I have in mind for Gwendolen. It is up to Algernon to choose for himself, of course. (*Pulls out her watch and studies the time.*) Come, dear. (**Gwendolen** *rises*) - We must have already missed five, if not six trains. If we miss any more trains, that might lead us to comment on the platform.

Enter Dr. **Chasuble**.

Chasuble: Everything is ready and in order for the christenings, gentlemen.

Lady Bracknell: The christenings, sir! Is that not somewhat premature?

Chasuble (*looking rather puzzled, and pointing to* **Jack** *and* **Algernon**): But both these gentlemen have expressed the desire to be baptised immediately.

Lady Bracknell: At their age? The idea is both irreligious and grotesque. Algernon, I absolutely forbid you to be baptised at this age. I refuse to hear of such excess on your part. Lord Bracknell would be greatly displeased if he came to know that you wasted your time and money in such a way.

Chasuble: Am I to understand that there will be no christenings this afternoon then?

Jack: As matters do stand right now, I do not think that it would be of much practical value to either of us, Dr. Chasuble.

Chasuble: Such sentiments coming from you grieve me greatly, Mr. Worthing. The heretical views of the Anabaptists are savoured by them, views that I have completely disproved of in four of my unpublished sermons. However, considering that your present mood appears to be one that is weirdly secular, I shall return to the church at once. I have just been informed by the pew-opener that Miss Prism has been waiting for me in the vestry for the last hour and a half.

Lady Bracknell: (*starting*): Miss Prism! Did I just hear you say a Miss Prism?

Chasuble: Yes, you did, Lady Bracknell. In fact, I am on my way to join her now.

Lady Bracknell: Please allow me to detain you just for a moment. This matter might prove to be of the most vital importance as far as both Lord Bracknell and I are concerned. Now, pray tell me, is this Miss Prism a female who is repulsive, and remotely associated with education?

Chasuble (*in an indignant manner*): Why, she is the most cultivated of ladies I have ever seen. In fact, she is the very epitome of respectability.

Lady Bracknell: I think that it is obvious that it is the same person. May I ask what position she holds in your household?

Chasuble (*in a severe manner*): Madam, I am a celibate.

Jack (*interposing*): Lady Bracknell, allow me to explain. Miss Prism has been Miss Cardew's esteemed governess and trusted companion for a period of three years now.

Lady Bracknell: Despite what I hear of her, I must see her at once. Please let her be sent for immediately.

Chasuble (*looking off*): She approaches as we speak.

Enter **Miss Prism** hurriedly.

Miss Prism: Dear Canon, I was informed that you expected me in the vestry. I have been waiting there for an hour and three-quarters. (*She catches sight of* **Lady Bracknell**, *who has fixed her with a stony glare.* **Miss Prism** *turns pale and quails. She looks round in an anxious manner as if she desires to escape the room.*)

Lady Bracknell (*in a stern, judicial voice*): Prism! (**Miss Prism** *hangs her head in shame.*) Come here, Prism! (**Miss Prism** *approaches her in a humble manner.*) Prism! Where is that baby? Answer me! (*General shock.* **Canon** *starts back in horror.* **Algernon** *and* **Jack** *pretend to anxiously shield* **Cecily** *and* **Gwendolen** *from hearing*

the intricate details of a terrible public scandal.)
It was exactly twenty years ago, Prism, that
you left Lord Bracknell's house, Number
104, Upper Grosvenor Street, in charge of a
perambulator that contained a baby of the male
sex. Prism, you never returned! A few weeks
later, thanks to the thorough investigations of
the metropolitan police, the perambulator in
question was discovered at midnight. It was
standing by itself in a remote corner of Bayswater.
A manuscript was found inside it; the manuscript
of a three-volume novel of more than usually
revolting sentimentality. (**Miss Prism** *starts in
involuntary indignation.*) But the baby was not
there. (*Everyone in the room stares at* **Miss Prism**)
Prism! Where is that baby? (*A pause.*)

Miss Prism: I must admit with shame that I
do not know where the baby is. I only wish
that I did. Let me tell you the plain facts of
the case. On the morning of the day that you

have mentioned, a day that is branded in my memory forever, I prepared to take the baby out as usual on its perambulator. I also had in my possession a somewhat old, spacious handbag in which I had intended to carry the manuscript of a work of fiction that I had written in the hours that I was unoccupied. In a moment of absent-mindedness and mental distraction, for which I can never forgive myself, I deposited the manuscript in the perambulator, and placed the baby in the handbag instead.

Jack (*who has been listening attentively all this while*): But where did you deposit this handbag?

Miss Prism: Oh, Mr. Worthing, do not ask me.

Jack: Miss Prism, this is not a matter of small importance for me. I absolutely insist on knowing where you deposited that particular handbag containing that infant.

Miss Prism: I left it in the cloakroom of one of the larger railway stations of London.

Jack: What railway station?

Miss Prism: (*totally crushed*): Victoria. The Brighton Line. (*Sinks into a chair.*)

Jack: I must retire to my room for a moment. Gwendolen, please wait here for me.

Gwendolen: I will wait here for you all my life, if you are not too long that is.

Exit **Jack** in great excitement.

Chasuble: What do you think all this means, Lady Bracknell?

Lady Bracknell: I do not dare to even suspect what it means, Dr. Chasuble. I don't need to tell you that in families of high position strange coincidences are not supposed to take place. They are hardly considered appropriate.

Noises are heard overhead as if someone was throwing trunks about. Everyone looks up.

Cecily: Uncle Jack seems to be in a strange kind of agitation.

Chasuble: Your guardian has a nature that is

very emotional, Miss Cardew.

Lady Bracknell: I think that this noise is rather unpleasant. It appears as if he is having an argument with someone. I just hate arguments of any kind. They are mostly vulgar, and often convincing.

Chasuble (looking up): Ah, the noise has stopped now. (The noise is redoubled all of a sudden.)

Lady Bracknell: I really wish that he would arrive at a conclusion.

Gwendolen: Oh, the suspense is terrible to say the least. I hope it will last.

Enter **Jack** *with a black leather handbag in his hand.*

Jack (*rushing over to* **Miss Prism**): Miss Prism, is this the handbag? Do examine it carefully before you answer the question. Keep in mind that the happiness of more than one life is fully dependent on your reply.

Miss Prism (*calmly*): Well, it seems to be mine. Yes, of course, here is the injury it received because of the upsetting of a Gower Street omnibus in younger and happier times. Look! Here is the stain on the lining that was caused by the explosion of a temperance beverage, an incident I recall had taken place at Leamington. And right here, on the lock, are my initials. It had escaped my mind that had them placed there in a rather extravagant mood once. Yes, this bag undoubtedly belongs to me. I am delighted that it has been so unexpectedly restored to me. What a great inconvenience it has been being without it all these years.

Jack (*in a voice that is totally pathetic*): Much more is restored to you than this handbag, Miss Prism. I was the baby that you placed in it.

Miss Prism (*totally amazed*): You?

Jack (*embracing her*): Yes...mother!

Miss Prism (*recoiling in indignant astonishment*):

228

I am unmarried, Mr. Worthing.

Jack: Unmarried? Well, I must confess that this is a serious blow. But then again, who has the right to cast a stone against one that has faced much suffering? But cannot repentance wipe out an act of folly? Why indeed, should there be one law for men, and another for women? Mother, I forgive you. (*Tries to embrace her again*)

Miss Prism (*even more indignant now*): Mr. Worthing, there is some serious error. (*Pointing to* **Lady Bracknell**): There is the lady who can really tell you who you really are.

Jack (*after a pause*): Lady Bracknell, I hate to appear overtly inquisitive, but would you kindly tell me who I am?

Lady Bracknell: I am afraid that the news you are about to receive will not please you altogether. You are the son of my poor sister, Mrs. Moncrief, and you are as a result, Algernon's elder brother.

Jack: Algy's elder brother! Oh, then I have a

brother after all. I always knew I had a brother! Cecily, how on earth could you have ever doubted that I have a brother! (*Catches hold of* **Algernon**) Dr. Chasuble, meet my unfortunate brother. Miss Prism, here is my unfortunate brother. Gwendolen, Algy is my unfortunate brother. Algy, you young scoundrel, you must treat me with more respect in the near future. Why Algy, you have never behaved in a brotherly manner towards me in all your life.

Algernon: Well, I admit I did not till today, old boy. I did my best, however, although I daresay I was out of practice. (*Shakes hands*)

Gwendolen (*to* **Jack**): My own! But what own are you? What is your Christian name? What is it now that you have become someone else?

Jack: Good heavens! I had completely forgotten about that point. I suppose your decision on the subject of my name is irreversible?

Gwendolen: Well, I never change, except in my affections.

Cecily: What a noble nature you possess, Gwendolen.

Jack: Then we must clear up the question at once! One moment, Aunt Augusta. Tell me something, had I been christened already when Miss Prism left me in that handbag?

Lady Bracknell: You had been blessed with every luxury that money could possibly buy, including christening, by your loving and doting parents.

Jack: Then I was christened after all! That matter is settled. Now, tell me, what name was I given? Tell me! I am prepared for the worst.

Lady Bracknell: Well, being the eldest son of your parents, you were naturally christened after your father.

Jack (*irritably*): Yes, yes. But what was my father's Christian name?

Lady Bracknell (*meditatively*): Well, I cannot recall presently what the General's Christian

name was. But I have no doubt whatsoever that he had one. I admit that he was an eccentric man, but that was only in his later years. That was the result of the Indian climate, and marriage, and indigestion, and other things of a similar nature.

Jack: Algy! Don't you remember what our father's Christian name was?

Algernon: My dear boy, we were not even on speaking terms. You see, the old man died before I was a year old.

Jack: I suppose his name would be there in the Army Lists of the period. What do you think, Aunt Augusta?

Lady Bracknell: The General was generally a man of peace, with the exception of his domestic life, of course. But I have no doubt that his name would appear in any military directory.

Jack: Well, the army lists of the last forty years are here with me. I should have studied these delightful records constantly. (*Rushes to the bookcase and almost tears the books out*) M. Generals...Mallam, Maxbohm, Magley, what ghastly names they have- Markby, Migsby, Mobbs, Moncrieff!! Lieutenant 1840, Captain, Lieutenant-Colonel, Colonel, General 1869, Christian names, **Ernest John**. (*Puts the book down very quietly and speaks in a very calm manner*) There, I always told you, Gwendolen, that my name was Ernest, didn't I? Well, it is Ernest after all! I mean it is Ernest naturally!

Lady Bracknell: Yes, now I recall that the General was called Ernest. I knew that I had some particular reason for disliking that name.

Gwendolen: Ernest! My own Ernest! I felt right from the beginning that you could have no other name other than Ernest!

Jack: Gwendolen, I must admit that it is a terrible thing for a man to discover suddenly that throughout his life he has been speaking nothing but the truth. Can you forgive me, dear?

Gwendolen: Of course I can. For I feel that you are sure to change.

Jack: My own one!

Chasuble (*to* **Miss Prism**): Laetitia! (*Embraces her*)

Miss Prism (*enthusiastically*): Frederick! At last!

Algernon: Cecily! (*Embraces her*) At last!

Jack: Gwendolen! (Embraces her) At last!

Lady Bracknell: My dear nephew, you appear to be displaying signs of triviality.

Jack: On the contrary, Aunt Augusta, I have now realised for the first time in my life the vital Importance of Being Earnest.

About the Author

■ Oscar Wilde

Oscar Wilde was an Irish poet and playwright. He was born Oscar Fingal O'Flahertie Wills Wilde on October 16, 1854, at 21 Westland Row, Dublin, Ireland. His father, Sir William Wilde, was an eminent Victorian and an eye and ear surgeon. An author, playwright and poet, Oscar Wilde was a popular literary figure in late Victorian England. He was famous for his brilliant wit, flamboyant style and his works of fiction. After graduating from Oxford University, he lectured as a poet, art critic and a leading proponent of the principles of aestheticism. In 1891, he published *The Picture of Dorian Gray*, his only novel which was panned as immoral by Victorian critics, but is now considered one of his most notable works. As a dramatist, many of Wilde's plays were well received, including his satirical comedies *Lady Windermere's Fan* (1892), *A Woman of No Importance* (1893), *An Ideal Husband* (1895) and *The Importance of Being Earnest* (1895), his most famous play.

■ List of Main Characters

John (Jack/Ernest) Worthing - The play's protagonist, Jack Worthing is a young man who leads a double life. In Hertfordshire, in his country estate, he is known as Jack. In London he is known as Ernest. As a baby, Jack was discovered in a handbag in the cloakroom of Victoria Station by an old man who adopted him and subsequently made Jack guardian to his granddaughter, Cecily Cardew. Jack is in love with his friend Algernon's cousin, Gwendolen Fairfax.

Algernon Moncrieff - Algernon is a charming, idle, decorative bachelor, nephew of Lady Bracknell, cousin of Gwendolen Fairfax, and best friend of Jack Worthing, whom he has known for years as Ernest. Algernon is brilliant, witty, selfish, amoral, and given to making delightful paradoxical and epigrammatic pronouncements.

Gwendolen Fairfax - Algernon's cousin and Lady Bracknell's daughter, Gwendolen is in love with Jack, whom she knows as Ernest. A model and arbiter of high fashion and society, Gwendolen speaks with unassailable authority on matters of taste and morality. She is cosmopolitan and utterly pretentious. Gwendolen is fixated on the name Ernest and says she will not marry a man without that name.

Cecily Cardew - Jack's ward, the granddaughter of the old gentleman who found and adopted Jack when Jack was a baby. Cecily, like Gwendolen, is obsessed with the name Ernest. But she is even more intrigued by the idea of wickedness. This idea has prompted her to fall in love with Ernest in her imagination and to invent an elaborate romance and courtship between them.

Lady Bracknell - Algernon's snobbish, mercenary, and domineering aunt and Gwendolen's mother. Lady Bracknell married well and wants her daughter do the same. She is cunning, narrow-minded, and authoritarian.

■ Questions

- *How does Wilde show that Jack and Cecily have the same kinds of values?*

- *Judging by the tone in Earnest, what is Wilde's opinion of the aristocracy? Does he approve or disapprove of them?*

- *How do the aristocrats' values clash directly with a more standard concept of respectability?*

- *What is the importance of the city/country split? What qualities do city-dwellers usually have? How about country folks? Do these stereotypes work in Earnest?*

- *Wilde's play has two settings — the city of London and the country. How does he create differences between the two settings?*

- *What are the four main characters' relationships to reality? How do they cope, romanticise, or escape from it?*

- *What is the girls' fascination with the name "Ernest"? What does it have to do with their romantic idealisations? How are names used to indicate character (or not) in the play?*

- *What attitudes toward marriage do Wilde's characters explore?*

- *In what ways are the gender roles in Earnest reversed?*

- *Who is Dr. Chasuble? Describe him in detail.*

- *How are Miss Prism and Dr. Chasuble products of society? What does this reveal about Victorian attitudes towards education?*

- *How does Wilde create and comment on the differences between the social classes in England as represented by Lady Bracknell and the servants in both settings?*

- *By the end of the play, has Jack really learned the importance of being earnest? Why or why not?*

- *In the end, why doesn't Cecily care that Algernon's name isn't Ernest?*

- *How is conflict developed in the play?*